FÜN學

美國英語閱讀課本 7

各學科實用課文 二版

附 Workbook +MP3

AMERICAN SCHOOL TEXTBOOK

READING KEY

作者 Michael A. Putlack & e-Creative Contents　　譯者 丁宥暄

The Best Preparation for Building Academic Reading Skills and Vocabulary

The Reading Key series is designed to help students to understand American school textbooks and to develop background knowledge in a wide variety of academic topics. This series also provides learners with the opportunity to enhance their reading comprehension skills and vocabulary, which will assist them when they take various English exams.

Reading Key <Volume 1–3> is
a three-book series designed for beginner to intermediate learners.

Reading Key <Volume 4–6> is
a three-book series designed for intermediate to high-intermediate learners.

Reading Key <Volume 7–9> is
a three-book series designed for high-intermediate learners.

Features

- A wide variety of topics that cover American school subjects
  helps learners expand their knowledge of academic topics through interdisciplinary studies

- Intensive practice for reading skill development
  helps learners prepare for various English exams

- Building vocabulary by school subjects and themed texts
  helps learners expand their vocabulary and reading skills in each subject

- Graphic organizers for each passage
  show the structure of the passage and help to build summary skills

- Captivating pictures and illustrations related
  to the topics help learners gain a broader understanding
  of the topics and key concepts

Table of Contents

Chapter 2
Science

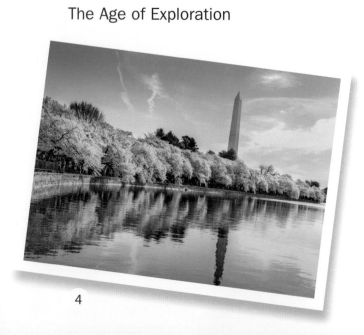

Chapter **3**
Mathematics • Language • Visual Arts • Music

Workbook for Daily Review

Subject	Topic & Area	Title
Social Studies ★ **History and Geography**	The U.S. Geography	The Regions of the United States
	People and Government	A Nation of Diversity
	The U.S. Economy	From Farming to Technology
	History and Culture	The Native People of North America
	World History	The Age of Exploration
	The American History	The Spanish Conquerors in the Americas
	The American History	The First French and English Colonies
	The American History	The American Revolution
Science	Classifying Living Things	The Five Kingdoms of Organisms
	Classifying Living Things	The Seven Levels of Classification
	A World of Plants	Plant Structures and Functions
	A World of Plants	Flowers and Seeds
	A World of Plants	Plants With Seeds
	A World of Plants	Seedless Vascular Plants and Nonvascular Plants
	A World of Plants	How Do Plants Respond to Their Environments?
Mathematics	Numbers and Number Sense	Understanding Numbers
	Geometry	Geometric Figures
Language and Literature	Literature	The *Iliad* and the *Odyssey*
	Language Arts	Figures of Speech
Visual Arts	Visual Arts	Greek and Roman Art
Music	A World of Music	The Western Musical Tradition

FÜN學

美國英語閱讀課本

各學科實用課文 二版

7

Workbook

AMERICAN SCHOOL TEXTBOOK

READING KEY

作者 Michael A. Putlack & e-Creative Contents 譯者 丁宥暄

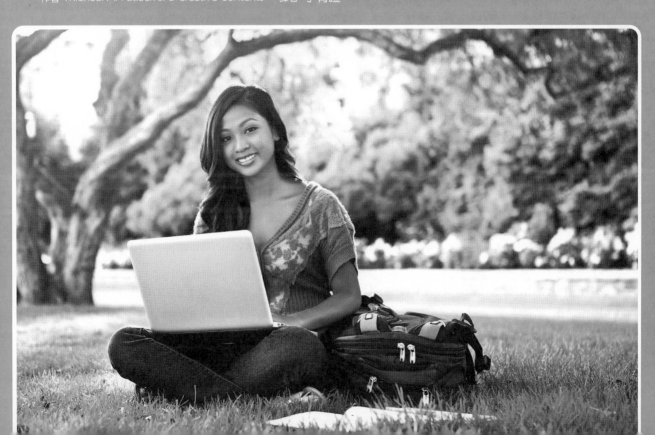

01 The Regions of the United States

🎧 22

A Listen to the passage and fill in the blanks.

1. The United States can be divided into five _____ regions. Each region has its own _____ environment, such as landforms and climate. These _____ set each region apart from the other ones.

2. The Northeast region includes 11 states and the nation's _____, Washington, D.C. (District of Columbia). The Atlantic Coastal Plain and _____ _____ are the Northeast's major landforms. The Northeast is often divided into two _____: New England and the Middle Atlantic States.

3. In American history, many of the first _____ from Europe settled in the Northeast. New England is known for the early settlements by the Pilgrims and _____. The Middle Atlantic has some of the most _____ populated areas and largest urban areas in the U.S., including New York City, Washington, D.C., and _____.

4. The Southeast includes _____ states. The Mississippi River _____ through the western part of the region. A warm climate and a long _____ _____ in the Southeast help farmers grow many different kinds of _____ _____. Tobacco and cotton were some of the first cash crops for early _____ owners. Peaches in Georgia and oranges in sunny _____ are two important cash crops for modern Southeast farmers.

5. The Midwest is a region of plains and _____. The Great Plains and the Central Plains are known for their rich fields of corn, soybeans, and wheat that _____ as far as the eye can see. The Mississippi River begins there, and four of the _____ _____ are in the Midwest. Its flat land and fertile _____ make this region a center for agriculture. People often call the Midwest "the _____ of the United States."

6. The Southwest includes Arizona, New Mexico, Texas, and _____. The region has many _____ and range areas, so it contains several deserts. There are also numerous _____, canyons, mesas, and buttes. The Grand Canyon, one of the best-known _____ in the U.S., is located in the Southwest.

7. Finally, the West includes California, Nevada, Oregon, _____, and the Mountain States. Alaska and _____ are in the western region, but they are separate from the _____ United States. The region is a _____ area with many different environments. The Northwest is known for its long _____ along the Pacific Ocean _____ the Southwest is dry and contains many deserts. Much of the Mountain States is _____ by the Rocky Mountains.

B Complete each sentence with the correct word. Change the form if necessary.

> metropolitan   landform   stretch   dominate   rainfall

1 The physical environment of a region includes its _____ and climate.

2 The continental United States _____ from Canada to Mexico.

3 Arid regions get very little _____ all throughout the year.

4 New York City is a large _____ area with millions of people.

5 The Midwest region is _____ by croplands.

C Write the meaning of each word and phrase from Word List (main book p.104) in English.

1 地理的 _____

2 自然環境 _____

3 將……分開 _____

4 哥倫比亞特區 _____

5 大西洋沿岸平原 _____

6 山脈 _____

7 子區域 _____

8 以……而聞名 _____

9 西元 1620 年搭乘五月花號（*Mayflower*）
移居美洲的英國清教徒 _____

10 清教徒 _____

11 人口密度高的 _____

12 城市的 _____

13 大都市的 _____

14 生長季 _____

15 經濟作物 _____

16 大農場 _____

17 大草原；牧場 _____

18 延伸 _____

19 視線所及 _____

20 北美五大湖 _____

21 肥沃的 _____

22 農田 _____

23 農業 _____

24 產糧區；麵包籃 _____

25 乾燥的 _____

26 為數眾多的 _____

27 多樣的 _____

28 高聳於；俯視 _____

▶ A、C 大題解答請參照主冊課文及 Word List（主冊 p. 104）
B 大題解答請見本書 P. 44 Answer Key

02 The United States
A Nation of Diversity

🎧 23

A Listen to the passage and fill in the blanks.

1. The United States is sometimes called a nation of _____. People from many different countries and _____ live there. It took _____ for the United States to become a _____ society. And the country's people did not come from _____ _____ the world at the _____ _____. In fact, _____ to America happened in various stages.

2. After Christopher Columbus discovered America in _____, many Europeans started to move to America. The first _____ to come to America were English, Germans, Irish, _____, and French. Many _____ started coming as well. But they were _____, so they were _____ to America against their will.

3. Then, between 1880 and _____, a second wave of immigrants _____ _____ the United States. Many of these _____ came from _____ and Eastern European countries, including Italy, _____, and Russia. Since the late _____, Asian immigrants—people from China, Japan, Korea, and other countries—have _____ _____ the western United States.

4. While the first immigrants often _____ _____ to rural areas, later immigrants _____ _____ the cities. For instance, New York and Boston were _____ to Italian and _____ immigrants, the largest _____ _____ in the second _____ _____ immigrants. Chicago was home to _____ _____ _____ many races and nationalities.

5. Today, the United States has _____ from almost every country. But not all _____ have always gotten along with each other. Immigrants sometimes encountered _____. Early immigrants, such as English settlers, _____, and Germans, _____ much with English culture. However, _____ immigrants were very different. They spoke different _____ and had different _____ and customs. Some people who were already well settled _____ more poor newcomers _____. As a result, social discrimination _____ blacks, Jews, _____, and other ethnic groups continued into the _____.

6. However, the U.S. _____ passed laws to end discrimination in the _____. Now, all people are treated _____ no matter what race they are. So, most Americans live together _____ _____.

B Complete each sentence with the correct word. Change the form if necessary.

| as a result   stream into   ethnic group   discrimination   race |

1 Immigrants _____ _____ the vast empty land in the United States in the 1800s.

2 _____ ___ _____ of the new laws, discrimination is now illegal.

3 An _____ _____ is a group of people who have the same customs, language, and history.

4 In the late 1800s, many of the new immigrants faced _____.

5 Chicago was home to a mixture of many _____ and nationalities.

C Write the meaning of each word and phrase from Word List in English.

1 移民國家 _____

2 種族 _____

3 世紀 _____

4 多元文化社會 _____

5 同時 _____

6 移民 _____

7 在不同的階段 _____

8 違背某人的意願 _____

9 湧入 _____

10 新來的人 _____

11 流入 _____

12 散布 _____

13 集中在某處 _____

14 猶太人的 _____

15 族群 _____

16 國籍 _____

17 與……和睦相處 _____

18 遭受 _____

19 歧視 _____

20 對待 _____

21 公平地 _____

22 無論什麼 _____

23 和諧 _____

03 The U.S. Economy
From Farming to Technology

⌒ 24

A Listen to the passage and fill in the blanks.

1. An economy is the way that _____ and services are produced and _____.
The economy of a country includes the _____ of all producers and
_____ within that country. A strong _____ produces many goods
and services.

2. Today, the _____ domestic product (GDP) of the United States is the _____
_____ any country in the world. The GDP is the _____ _____ of goods
and services produced within a country in a year. So having the highest _____ in
the world _____ that the U.S. has the largest economy in the world.

3. The early American economy was _____ _____ farming. The majority of
colonists who came to America from Europe in the 1600s and _____ were farmers.
Later, the _____ and service industries _____ _____ the largest
parts of the economy. Today, the _____ and technology industries are the
_____ parts of the economy.

4. In the United States, people and companies are part of a _____ _____
economy. In a free market, people choose what to produce and _____ _____
_____. Farmers decide what _____ to plant. Factory owners decide what
products to _____. _____ decide what kinds of products to
sell. And consumers consider _____ _____ when they make decisions
about buying these goods and _____. People can choose how they _____ and
spend their money without government _____. The American economy is
also based on the _____ system. This means that people can own and run
their own _____. People who start and run their own businesses are called
_____.

5. In most _____, people who sell goods or services decide on their prices according
to the _____ _____ supply and demand. If the supply is large yet _____ is
low, the price usually _____ _____. If the supply is _____ or small yet
demand is high, then the price often _____.

B Complete each sentence with the correct word. Change the form if necessary.

> scarce   free market   free-enterprise   entrepreneur   supply

1 In a _____ _____, people choose what to produce and what to buy.

2 The American economy is based on the _____ system.

3 People decide on their prices according to the law of _____ and demand.

4 When some products are _____, their prices increase.

5 A person who starts his or her own business is called an _____.

C Write the meaning of each word and phrase from Word List in English.

1 分發；分銷 _____

2 生產者 _____

3 消費者 _____

4 經濟 _____

5 國內生產總值；國內生產毛額

_____

6 根基於 _____

7 大多數 _____

8 殖民地開拓者；殖民地居民

_____

9 製造業 _____

10 金融業 _____

11 科技業 _____

12 發展最迅速的 _____

13 自由市場經濟 _____

14 製造 _____

15 商店老闆 _____

16 考慮 _____

17 機會成本 _____

18 做決定 _____

19 干涉 _____

20 自由企業制度 _____

21 經營某人自己的事業 _____

22 企業家；創業者 _____

23 大多數情況下 _____

24 供需法則 _____

25 下降 _____

26 缺乏的 _____

The Native People of North America

🎧 25

A Listen to the passage and fill in the blanks.

1. Around _____ years ago, the first _____ _____ arrived in the Americas. Many _____ believe they crossed a land bridge from Asia.

2. During the Ice Age, there was _____ _____ of land that connected Asia and North America. From Asia, big _____ of animals moved across that _____ _____ looking for food, and the first people _____ the animals that supplied their food. During their _____ _____, they also _____ wild berries, nuts, and fruits for food. That is why we call them _____.

3. As the years _____, more and more people _____ _____ the land bridge, and they spread all over the Americas. These people were the _____ of the Native Americans. Over time, early Native Americans began to _____ _____ and to build homes. They _____ _____ various places and built _____.

4. Many Native American _____ adapted to their environments. Cultures developed _____ _____ the climate and the natural resources of the tribes' _____. This _____ each tribe to live differently from the others.

5. In the _____ _____ area of North America, there were tribes like the Sioux and Lakota. They hunted _____ for food and _____ the land. They lived in _____, cone-shaped tents that they could _____ from place to place.

6. In the Southwest, there were tribes such as the _____ and Navajo. They adapted to the harsh, arid _____ in the desert. The Pueblo _____ in the desert using a method called _____ _____. They built homes, called pueblos, out of _____. Adobe protected their homes from _____ heat and cold.

7. In the West, the _____ in Alaska hunted _____ for food and clothing. The Tlingit were skilled _____ _____. They used wood to make totem poles, _____, and crafts.

8. And in the East, the Iroquois built longhouses using materials from the forests. Some tribes even formed an _____ called the Iroquois Confederacy. They were among the first Native Americans to _____ _____ European colonists when they arrived in _____ _____.

B Complete each sentence with the correct word. Change the form if necessary.

> wander   archaeologist   ancestor   adapt   civilization

1 The _____ of the Native Americans were the people who crossed the land bridge.

2 The Native Americans had their own _____.

3 Many Native American tribes _____ to the harsh environment.

4 Some tribes _____ the land in search of food.

5 An _____ is a person who studies past human civilizations.

C Write the meaning of each word and phrase from Word List in English.

1 原住民 _____

2 考古學家 _____

3 陸橋 _____

4 狹長陸地 _____

5 畜群 _____

6 狩獵旅行 _____

7 採集 _____

8 採獵者 _____

9 祖先 _____

10 美洲原住民 _____

11 文明 _____

12 部落 _____

13 適應 _____

14 環境 _____

15 流浪；漫遊 _____

16 梯皮（美國印第安人的圓錐形帳篷）
_____

17 圓錐形的 _____

18 嚴酷的 _____

19 旱作 _____

20 用……作材料 _____

21 曬乾的泥磚 _____

22 極端的 _____

23 鯨 _____

24 工藝工作者 _____

25 圖騰柱 _____

26 獨木舟 _____

27 工藝品（多用複數形） _____

28 同盟；結盟 _____

29 易洛魁聯盟 _____

30 與……交易 _____

🎧 26

A Listen to the passage and fill in the blanks.

1 In the _____ century, many European countries, such as _____, Spain, France, and England, traded for _____ from Asia. Gold, silk, and _____ from India and China were in great _____ in Europe. Europeans were _____ ____ pay high prices for Asia's goods. However, it took a very long time for _____ to travel to Asia by land. So the Europeans began to _____ _____ another _____ to Asia.

2 The Europeans _____ _____ find sea routes to Asia. Portugal _____ the way. The _____ developed a new ship, called the _____, which could sail farther and _____ than other ships. In 1418, Prince Henry the _____, a Portuguese prince, began sending _____ to explore the western coast of Africa. Slowly, but _____, the Portuguese sailed _____ and farther south. Finally, in _____, the Portuguese captain Bartolomeu Dias became the first European to _____ the southern tip of Africa, the _____ _____ _____ _____. But he did not enter the _____ _____. Around ten years _____, Vasco da Gama sailed all the way from Portugal to _____. The Europeans had discovered a _____ to Asia.

3 The Portuguese sailed to Asia by _____ _____ Africa. But Christopher Columbus, an Italian, believed he could _____ Asia by sailing west across the _____ _____. He _____ Ferdinand and Isabella, the king and _____ of Spain, to _____ a three-ship mission. With his ships the *Pinta*, *Niña*, and *Santa María*, he _____ _____ in _____. After _____ weeks, his crew _____ land. It was not India _____; it was the New World. Columbus had _____ North and South America.

4 In _____, an expedition _____ _____ Ferdinand Magellan set sail from Spain. Magellan was killed in the _____, but his crew achieved the first _____ of the world in _____. Soon _____, the French, Dutch, and English entered the race of global _____, too.

5 The Europeans' sea explorations to reach Asia during the fifteenth and _____ centuries changed the world _____. We call this time "the _____ _____ Exploration" or "the Age of _____."

B Complete each sentence with the correct word. Change the form if necessary.

> round   Age of Exploration   sponsor   compete to   circumnavigation

1 During the Age of Discovery, the Europeans _____ _____ find sea routes to Asia.

2 Most explorers needed someone to _____ their expeditions with money.

3 It took many trips before the Portuguese could _____ the southern tip of Africa.

4 Ferdinand Magellan's crew achieved the first _____ of the world in 1522

5 The Europeans' sea explorations during the 15th and 16th centuries are called "the _____ _____ _____."

C Write the meaning of each word and phrase from Word List in English.

1 十五世紀 _____

2 香料 _____

3 需求量大 _____

4 樂意；願意 _____

5 付高價 _____

6 商人 _____

7 由陸路 _____

8 尋找 _____

9 路線 _____

10 爭相做某事 _____

11 海路 _____

12 領路；打先鋒 _____

13 葡萄牙人；葡萄牙的 _____

14 卡拉維爾帆船；輕快帆船 _____

15 更遠地 _____

16 航海家亨利王子 _____

17 探險隊；遠征隊 _____

18 平穩地 _____

19 繞行 _____

20 非洲南端 _____

21 好望角 _____

22 水路 _____

23 說服 _____

24 資助 _____

25 任務 _____

26 啟航 _____

27 環球航行 _____

28 不久之後 _____

29 大航海時代 _____

30 地理大發現 _____

06 The Spanish Conquerors in the Americas

🎧 27

A Listen to the passage and fill in the blanks.

1. After _____ discovery of America, more and more _____ came to the New World. Most came _____ _____ _____ gold, silver, and other treasures. They _____ _____ make Spain the richest country in Europe. There were _____ already in the Americas, of course, but the Spaniards _____ the rights of the local people.

2. In the sixteenth _____, there were two major _____ in Central and South America. One was the _____ Empire in the land in _____ Mexico. And the _____ Empire was in the South American land that is _____ today. Both the _____ and the Incas had a lot of gold and other _____ that the Spaniards wanted.

3. In order to establish _____ in South America, Spain needed to _____ the Aztecs first. In _____, Hernando Cortés sailed to Mexico with about 550 _____. After just a few years, in _____, the Spanish _____ the Aztec capital Tenochtitlan and _____ the Aztec Empire. A _____ later, in _____, another Spanish conquistador, Francisco Pizarro, _____ the Inca Empire. Pizarro _____ an expedition with only _____ men and 37 horses.

4. The Aztecs were _____ warriors, and the Incas were strong people, too. And the Spaniards had many _____ soldiers. So why did the _____ win? They had much stronger _____ like guns, _____, and metal _____. They _____ _____, too, which the Native Americans had never seen before. The Spanish also had one more _____ weapon: _____. The Spanish arrived in the New World with _____ diseases like _____. The Native Americans had no _____ to these diseases, so _____ _____ them died. As a result, the Spanish easily _____ most Native American _____. Then, they _____ the natives and took their treasures. Spain also _____ a lot of land in North and South America and _____ _____ colonies.

B Complete each sentence with the correct word. Change the form if necessary.

> Inca Empire   enslave   in search of   Aztec Empire   smallpox

1 Spaniards came to the New World _____ _____ _____ gold, silver, and other treasures.

2 In the sixteenth century , there was the _____ _____ in the land in modern-day Mexico.

3 The _____ _____ was in the South American land that is Peru today.

4 _____ and other diseases killed large numbers of Native Americans.

5 The Spanish _____ the natives and took their treasures.

C Write the meaning of each word and phrase from Word List in English.

1 西班牙人 _____

2 尋找 _____

3 開始；著手 _____

4 忽視 _____

5 權利 _____

6 當地居民 _____

7 今日的 _____

8 財富 _____

9 建立 _____

10 殖民地 _____

11 征服 _____

12 征服者 _____

13 捕捉 _____

14 結束 _____

15 十年 _____

16 兇猛的 _____

17 武器 _____

18 槍 _____

19 火砲 _____

20 盔甲 _____

21 騎馬 _____

22 致命的 _____

23 疾病 _____

24 可怕的 _____

25 天花 _____

26 免疫力 _____

27 擊敗 _____

28 奴役 _____

29 聲稱 _____

30 建立 _____

07 Colonial America
The First French and English Colonies

🎧 28

A Listen to the passage and fill in the blanks.

1 While the Spanish _____ _____ Central and South America, people from other European countries explored and _____ North America. On the _____ _____, the two most important countries were France and _____.

2 The French mostly explored the area that is _____ today. In _____, Jacques Cartier _____ _____ the St. Lawrence River. Other French explorers, such as Sieur de La Salle, explored the _____ _____ North America. La Salle discovered the _____ _____ and claimed it for _____. In 1608, Samuel de Champlain built a _____ French settlement in present-day _____.

3 The English mostly _____ _____ the eastern part of the continent along the _____ _____. The first permanent English _____ was founded at Jamestown, Virginia, in _____. The _____ came there to _____ their fortune. They wanted to _____ _____. But there was no gold, and many settlers _____ _____ hunger and disease. However, _____ _____ leaders like John Smith, who was saved by Pocahontas, the daughter of an Indian chief, Jamestown grew bigger and _____.

4 In _____, another important English settlement was _____ in present-day Massachusetts. It was started by the _____. They sailed on the *Mayflower* and landed in _____, Massachusetts. They left England because of their religious _____.

5 Some other English colonists _____ the Pilgrims. They were the _____. Like the Pilgrims, the Puritans were a _____ religious group of _____. The Puritans settled in the area of present-day Boston, _____.

6 Over the _____ _____, many more people moved from Europe to America. Most came from England, but some also came from France, _____, and other countries. _____, they founded thirteen _____ colonies. Every colony was on _____ _____ _____ of the Atlantic. Later, these thirteen colonies would become the first _____ _____ the United States.

Complete each sentence with the correct word. Change the form if necessary.

permanent   Quebec   settlement   Puritan   the east coast   separate

1 In 1608, the French built a _____ French settlement in present-day _____.

2 The first permanent English _____ was founded at Jamestown, Virginia, in 1607.

3 _____ were a deeply religious group of Christians who came from England.

4 Eventually, the English founded thirteen _____ colonies.

5 Every English colony was on _____ _____ _____ of the Atlantic Ocean.

C Write the meaning of each word and phrase from Word List in English.

1   集中於   _____   13 繁榮   _____

2   將……開拓為殖民地 _____   14 西元1620年搭乘五月花號（*Mayflower*）

3   內部   _____   移居美洲的英國清教徒

4   永久的   _____   _____

5   殖民地   _____   15 信仰   _____

6   定居於   _____   16 清教徒   _____

7   建立於   _____   17 強烈地   _____

8   尋找   _____   18 宗教的   _____

9   財富   _____   19 基督徒   _____

10 致富   _____   20 荷蘭   _____

11 幸虧   _____   21 最後；終於   _____

12 印地安酋長   _____   22 獨立的   _____

🎧 29

A Listen to the passage and fill in the blanks.

1 In the _____, there were thirteen English _____ in America. A colony is an area _____ _____ the government of another country. The thirteen colonies in America were ruled by the _____ of England.

2 Meanwhile, from 1756 to _____, England and France fought the _____ _____ _____. England gained the land east of the Mississippi River by _____ the war. However, the _____ was very expensive for England. _____ _____ _____ wanted the thirteen American colonies to help _____ _____ the government's debt. He made laws the _____ did not like and began to tax goods.

3 In 1764, the English _____ passed the Sugar Act, and it passed the Stamp Act in _____. This meant that when the colonists bought sugar, _____, and paper, they had to pay _____ money. The colonists _____. They called them the _____ _____ and began _____ English goods. They said, "No _____ without representation." They wanted _____ in Parliament, but the king refused. Soon, fighting began _____ the English and the colonists.

4 Many Americans wanted _____ from England. _____ between the Americans and English soldiers led to the Boston Massacre in _____. American _____ began training to be ready to fight "at a minute's notice." On April 19, _____, English soldiers, called _____, and American minutemen _____ _____ Lexington and Concord, Massachusetts. These were the first two battles of the _____ _____. One year later, on July 4, _____, the Continental Congress signed the _____ _____ _____. They _____ that America was an independent country.

5 George Washington was _____ the commander of the Continental Army. The early years of the war were _____. After winning the Battle of Saratoga in _____, the Americans _____ France and other European countries to help them. There were many _____ _____ fighting. The Americans both won and lost _____. Then, in _____, the American army and French navy _____ General Cornwallis, the English army commander, to _____ at Yorktown, Virginia. The war was _____. Two years later, England _____ the _____ of the American colonies.

B Complete each sentence with the correct word. Change the form if necessary.

> boycott   pay off   representative   Declaration of Independence   colony

1 King George III wanted the thirteen American colonies to help _____ _____ the government's debt.

2 The colonists protested and began _____ English goods.

3 The Americans desired _____ in the British Parliament but were rejected.

4 In 1776, the Continental Congress signed the _____ _____ _____.

5 In 1783, England recognized the independence of the American _____.

C Write the meaning of each word and phrase from Word List in English.

1 1760年代 _____

2 被……統治 _____

3 其間 _____

4 七年戰爭 _____

5 清償 _____

6 債 _____

7 向……課稅 _____

8 英國國會 _____

9 《糖稅法》 _____

10 《印花稅法》 _____

11 額外的 _____

12 抗議 _____

13 不可容忍法令 _____

14 聯合抵制；杯葛 _____

15 課稅 _____

16 代表 _____

17 代表人 _____

18 拒絕 _____

19 獨立 _____

20 緊張局勢 _____

21 （美國獨立戰爭期間）命令一下立即應召 的民兵 _____

22 通知 _____

23 （美國獨立戰爭時期的）英國軍人， 因穿紅制服而得其名 _____

24 （美國）獨立戰爭 _____

25 大陸會議 _____

26 《獨立宣言》 _____

27 宣告 _____

28 指派 _____

29 大陸軍 _____

30 投降 _____

09 The Five Kingdoms of Organisms

🎧 30

A Listen to the passage and fill in the blanks.

1. Organisms are _____ _____ the characteristics they have _____ _____.
Ancient scientists grouped all living things as _____ plants or animals. However,
when the _____ was invented, scientists discovered many organisms that
needed new _____. Today, scientists _____ living things into
five large groups called _____. They are the Monera, Protista, _____,
Plantae, and Animalia kingdoms.

2. Members of the Monera Kingdom are very simple _____ organisms. They
can _____ _____ only with a microscope. They are also called prokaryotes. This
means that they _____ a _____ in their cells. _____ and certain
types of algae are in the Monera Kingdom. These organisms get nutrients by
_____ them through their _____ _____.

3. Organisms in the Protista, or Protist, Kingdom are also _____. Some
have animal _____, some have plant features, and some have features of both
plants and animals. Most are single celled, but some have _____ _____. They
include animallike _____ and plantlike algae. The cells in _____ contain
chloroplasts. This enables them to do _____ and to make their own food.

4. Organisms in the Fungi Kingdom are _____ _____. They include molds,
yeasts, and _____. Fungi are similar to plants, but they do not get their
_____ from photosynthesis. Instead, they _____ _____ the decaying
tissues of other organisms.

5. Members of the Plantae, or Plant, Kingdom are _____ organisms that
cannot move. They include _____, mosses, and flowering and non-flowering plants.
Plant cells contain _____, which makes them green. It also _____
them to use photosynthesis to make their own food.

6. Members of the Animalia, or Animal, Kingdom are multicellular _____ that
can move. They include insects, worms, fish, reptiles, _____, birds, and
_____. Animals cannot _____ their own food. _____, they eat
other organisms such as plants and animals to _____ their nutrition.

Complete each sentence with the correct word. Change the form if necessary.

| kingdom | Animalia | Protista | feed on | microscopic |

1 Scientists classify living things into five large groups called _____.

2 Organisms in the _____ Kingdom may have characteristics of plants or animals.

3 Many animals _____ _____ other animals for nourishment.

4 The _____ organisms can be seen only with a microscope.

5 The _____ Kingdom includes a wide variety of organisms, from tiny insects to big mammals.

C Write the meaning of each word and phrase from Word List in English.

1 根據……分類 _____

2 共同的 _____

3 （生物分類上的）界 _____

4 原核生物界 _____

5 原生生物界 _____

6 真菌界 _____

7 植物界 _____

8 動物界 _____

9 單細胞的 _____

10 原核生物 _____

11 缺少 _____

12 細胞核 _____

13 似動物的 _____

14 水藻；海藻 _____

15 似植物的 _____

16 只能從顯微鏡裡看到的；微小的

_____

17 阿米巴；變形蟲 _____

18 葉綠體 _____

19 使能夠 _____

20 光合作用 _____

21 多細胞的 _____

22 黴菌 _____

23 酵母（菌） _____

24 蘑菇；傘菌 _____

25 以……為食物 _____

26 腐爛 _____

27 多細胞的 _____

28 蕨類植物 _____

29 苔蘚植物 _____

30 葉綠素 _____

🎧 31

A Listen to the passage and fill in the blanks.

1. There may be _____ _____ organisms on the planet that we do not know anything about. If you discovered a new living thing, what would you _____ it? How would you _____ it? Long ago, scientists around the world had trouble _____ about the organisms they were studying. They _____ different languages, so they called the same _____ different names. Swedish scientist Carl Linnaeus _____ _____ _____ this problem. He grouped all organisms into seven _____ and gave them _____ names, so all scientists would understand the names. Today, we still use the _____ _____ as the basis for classifying living things.

2. Scientists now classify all living things into _____ levels. They are kingdom, _____, class, order, family, genus, and species. At each level, all organisms share _____ characteristics.

3. The highest level is _____. Each kingdom can contain several _____, each phylum can contain several classes, and _____ _____. The classification gets more _____ as it goes down.

4. All organisms _____ _____ one of five kingdoms: _____, Protista, Fungi, Plantae, and Animalia. The next _____ is the phylum. Organisms that belong to the same phylum have similar _____ _____. For instance, the Animalia Kingdom has _____ phyla. One is _____. Chordates are animals with _____.

5. Classes, orders, and _____ further divide organisms. In the *Chordata* phylum, there are several _____. They include mammals, _____, birds, amphibians, and fish. In the *Mammalia* class, animals may belong to certain orders _____ _____ the food they eat. So there are orders for _____, herbivores, and other types of animals. In the order *Carnivora*, there are families for animals such as dogs, cats, and _____.

6. The last two categories are genus and _____. A _____ is a group of organisms that is closely related. Species is the most _____ classification. Members of a species _____ at least one characteristic that no other organisms have.

7. The way an organism is classified _____ its scientific name. When scientists want to _____ an organism, they _____ use the genus and the species. The first part of the name tells its genus. The second part of the name tells its _____. For example, the scientific name for _____ _____ is *Homo sapiens*. _____ is the genus, and *sapiens* is the species.

8. Altogether, the way an organism is classified _____ a lot of information about it. It allows people to note the _____ and differences between various organisms.

B Complete each sentence with the correct word. Change the form if necessary.

> genus   depend on   specific   determine   precise   level

1 Scientists classify all living things into seven _____: kingdom, phylum, class, order, family, _____, and species.

2 Grouping organisms _____ _____ the traits they have.

3 The classification gets more _____ as it goes down.

4 Species is the most _____ classification for an organism.

5 The way an organism is classified _____ its scientific name.

C Write the meaning of each word and phrase from Word List in English.

1 命名；名稱 _____

2 處理 _____

3 拉丁語的 _____

4 林奈分類系統 _____

5 根據 _____

6 級別 _____

7 （生物分類上的）界 _____

8 （生物分類上的）門 _____

9 （生物分類上的）綱 _____

10 （生物分類上的）目 _____

11 （生物分類上的）科 _____

12 （生物分類上的）屬 _____

13 （生物分類上的）種 _____

14 特有的 _____

15 明確的 _____

16 體型呈現 _____

17 脊索動物門 _____

18 脊骨 _____

19 肉食性動物 _____

20 草食性動物 _____

21 相關的 _____

22 精確的 _____

23 明確說明 _____

24 通常；一般 _____

25 人類 _____

26 智人 _____

🎧 32

A Listen to the passage and fill in the blanks.

① All plants have basic _____. They need sunlight, water, air, and _____ to live and grow. To meet their needs, all plants have certain parts with the same _____.

② Plants have _____ that hold them in the ground. Roots help _____ a plant in the soil and _____ the plant from moving. Roots are _____ _____ absorbing water and minerals from the soil. The _____ of a root helps it absorb water and _____ and send them to the other parts of the plant.

③ In most plants, tiny _____ _____ take in water and minerals from the soil. The water and minerals pass through the root's _____ and enter the _____. Then, they move _____ through the xylem to the _____ _____ and to all the parts of the plant.

④ Stems _____ leaves and flowers. Some stems, like those on trees, are _____ and hard. Other stems, like _____ on flowers, are much smaller and soft. Yet all stems have the same basic parts for _____ the _____ system of plants. The xylem in the stem moves water and _____ up from the roots. The _____ moves food from the plant's leaves to all the parts of the plant.

⑤ Some stems do more than _____. Some stems, like in _____, store food for the plants to use later. In fact, the potatoes we eat are _____ stems. In addition, the stems of _____ store water during long dry _____ in the desert.

⑥ Leaves are the _____ parts of a plant. Leaves are green because they contain _____. Chlorophyll is _____ _____ chloroplasts. It lets plants _____ photosynthesis. This is the food-making _____ of plants. Plants need water, _____ _____, and sunlight to undergo photosynthesis. Inside the _____, water and carbon dioxide combine to make sugar and _____. The plants then use this _____ to live and grow. During photosynthesis, plants _____ oxygen into the air, so other organisms can _____ it. Then, during _____, which occurs in plants and animals, the water and carbon dioxide are released into _____ _____.

B Complete each sentence with the correct word. Change the form if necessary.

> part   function   responsible for   prevent   chloroplast   oxygen

1 All plants have certain _____ with the same _____ to meet their needs.

2 Plants' roots _____ them from being blown away by the wind.

3 The phloem is _____ _____ moving food to all of the parts of the plant.

4 _____ are necessary for a plant to undergo photosynthesis.

5 Water and carbon dioxide combine to make sugar and _____ inside the chloroplasts.

C Write the meaning of each word and phrase from Word List in English.

1 基本需要 _____

2 部分；部位；構造 _____

3 功能 _____

4 托住；支撐 _____

5 使固定 _____

6 防止…… _____

7 負責 _____

8 構造 _____

9 微小的 _____

10 根毛 _____

11 皮層 _____

12 木質部 _____

13 運輸系統 _____

14 韌皮部 _____

15 地下莖 _____

16 仙人掌 _____

17 進行 _____

18 過程 _____

19 二氧化碳 _____

20 糖 _____

21 氧氣 _____

22 釋放 _____

23 呼吸 _____

24 呼吸（作用） _____

12 Flowers and Seeds
How Do Plants Reproduce?

🎧 33

A Listen to the passage and fill in the blanks.

1 Most plants make _____ from their flowers. Flowers are the _____ organs in the plants. Thanks to them, plants can produce seeds that will develop and ___ _____ _____ new plants.

2 Flowers have _____ _____ and female parts. The male parts make _____. The female parts make _____ _____ that become seeds.

3 The _____ is a flower's male part. A stamen has two _____. The _____ produces pollen grains. The _____ is the stalk that connects the anther to the plant. The pistil is the flower's _____ _____. The _____ has three parts. At its top is the _____. The stigma captures the _____ _____ that fall on it. The stem-like part in the middle is the _____. The _____ is the base of the flower that contains egg cells. The egg cells develop into seeds if they are _____.

4 To make seeds, a plant must be _____ first. _____ occurs when a pollen grain is _____ from the anther to the stigma. This can happen through _____ or cross-pollination. If the pollen is _____ in the same flower, it is called self-pollination. If the pollen is transferred from the anther of one flower to the stigma of _____ flower, it is called _____. This is where the flower _____ are useful. Flower petals are the colorful _____ _____ of flowers. They attract bees, butterflies, _____, or other animals. As they go from flower to flower, some pollen gets _____ on them. The pollen then _____ transferred to other flowers. That is how many flowers get _____.

5 Once a flower gets pollinated, a _____ _____ starts to grow, and it _____ _____ into the ovary until it _____ an egg cell. Then, _____ occurs, and a seed forms. The seed contains an _____ of a new plant. The seed first develops into a _____, which may have one or more seeds. Many of these seeds _____ fall to the ground. When that happens, they may _____ and grow into new plants.

B Complete each sentence with the correct word. Change the form if necessary.

> transfer   fertilize   female   pollinate   pollen tube

1 Flowers have male parts and _____ parts.

2 Bees and hummingbirds are often responsible for _____ flowers.

3 If the pollen is _____ in the same flower, it is called self-pollination.

4 Once a flower gets pollinated, a _____ _____ starts to grow.

5 The egg cells develop into seeds if they are _____.

C Write the meaning of each word and phrase from Word List in English.

1 種子 _____

2 生殖器官 _____

3 雄性構造 _____

4 雌性構造 _____

5 花粉 _____

6 雄蕊 _____

7 花藥 _____

8 花絲 _____

9 柄 _____

10 雌蕊 _____

11 柱頭 _____

12 花柱 _____

13 子房 _____

14 受精 _____

15 被授花粉 _____

16 授粉（作用） _____

17 被轉移 _____

18 自花授粉 _____

19 異花授粉 _____

20 花瓣 _____

21 外層覆蓋物 _____

22 黏在……上 _____

23 花粉管 _____

24 受精（作用） _____

25 胚芽 _____

26 發芽 _____

Daily Test

13 Plants With Seeds

What Are Some Types of Plants?

🎧 34

A **Listen to the passage and fill in the blanks.**

1. The _____ of plants have seeds. There are two major groups of _____ _____:
angiosperms and gymnosperms.

2. Most plants on the earth are _____. Flowers, _____, crops, and most
trees are all angiosperms. Angiosperms, also known as _____ _____, produce
flowers and fruits. Their seeds are _____ by fruits. The fruit _____
the seeds inside it. Fruits of all angiosperms form from flowers, the plants'
_____ organs.

3. Scientists divide angiosperms into two groups that are _____ _____ how many
seed leaves a plant's seed has. Monocotyledons, or _____, have one seed leaf,
also called a _____. Dicotyledons, or dicots, have two _____ _____.

4. Angiosperms live in all _____ and in all parts of the world. They are the largest
_____ in the Plant Kingdom.

5. _____ produce seeds but have no flowers or fruits. The seeds are not
surrounded by a _____. They produce seeds on _____. Most gymnosperms
are evergreens and have narrow, _____ leaves. One kind of gymnosperm is the
_____, which includes pine, _____, and cypress trees. Cycads and
_____ are two other kinds of gymnosperms.

6. _____ _____ having flowers and fruits, gymnosperms _____ in
other ways. For example, conifers, such as _____ _____, often have both male
and female cones on a tree. Male cones release pollen grains, which contain _____
_____. The female cones produce _____ _____. When the pollen grains
_____ _____ by the wind and happen to land on a female cone, the _____
_____ from the pollen join with egg cells. The _____ eggs eventually
become a seed. When the seeds _____, the female cones fall from the tree and
_____ them on the ground. The wind or water often _____ the seeds away
from the tree. When the _____ are right, the seeds _____ and grow
into new pine trees.

7. Gymnosperms are the _____ seed plants. Millions of years ago, they were the
_____ plants on the earth. Today, there are only around _____ _____
of gymnosperms.

B Complete each sentence with the correct word. Change the form if necessary.

> division   female cone   dominant   seed plant   based on

1 There are two major groups of _____ _____: angiosperms and gymnosperms.

2 Scientists divide angiosperms into two groups that are _____ _____ how many seed leaves a plant's seed has.

3 Angiosperms are the largest _____ in the Plant Kingdom.

4 Conifers often have both male and _____ _____ on a tree.

5 Gymnosperms are no longer the most _____ plants on the planet.

C Write the meaning of each word and phrase from Word List in English.

1 大多數 _____

2 種子植物 _____

3 被子植物 _____

4 裸子植物 _____

5 開花植物 _____

6 根據 _____

7 子葉   s _____

8 單子葉植物 _____

9 子葉   c _____

10 雙子葉植物 _____

11 毬果 _____

12 常綠樹 _____

13 針狀的 _____

14 松柏科植物；針葉樹 _____

15 西洋杉 _____

16 柏樹 _____

17 蘇鐵 _____

18 銀杏 _____

19 成熟 _____

20 使分散 _____

21 帶走 _____

22 主要的 _____

14 Plants Without Seeds
Seedless Vascular Plants and Nonvascular Plants

🎧 35

A Listen to the passage and fill in the blanks.

1 Most plants _____ with seeds, but not all of them do. Some reproduce _____ using seeds. We can divide these _____ _____ into two groups: seedless vascular plants and seedless _____ plants.

2 Vascular plants have _____ _____ that are made of tubelike cells. These tissues let water and nutrients _____ _____ the roots and stems. All _____ and gymnosperms are vascular plants. Nonvascular plants, however, _____ these tissues.

3 Mosses are the most _____ types of seedless nonvascular plants. These plants all use photosynthesis to provide _____ for themselves. However, they lack the _____ that vascular plants have. This lack of veins _____ nonvascular plants from growing very large and also makes them grow _____ _____ the ground.

4 _____ are the most common type of seedless vascular plants. These are very old plants that once _____ millions of years ago. Ferns have leaves that are called _____. They grow from the underground stem called a _____. Ferns have vascular tissues, so they can grow tall and _____.

5 Both _____ and ferns reproduce without seeds. They use _____ to make new plants, so their life cycles are _____. Both mosses and ferns have two _____ stages in their life cycles.

6 Let's look at the _____ _____ of mosses. In the first _____, mosses produce spores _____. When the _____ _____ opens, the spores are released. Spores that land on _____ ground grow into new plants. This stage is called _____ reproduction. As mosses develop, they have male branches and female _____. The male branches produce _____, and the female branches produce eggs. When there is enough _____, the sperm cells move to the eggs and _____ them. Each fertilized egg produces a _____ that develops a capsule, called a spore case, which is filled with _____. This second stage is called _____ reproduction. The life cycle of ferns is very _____ _____ that of mosses.

B Complete each sentence with the correct word. Change the form if necessary.

| asexually   vascular tissue   sexual reproduction   lack   moisture |

1 Vascular plants have _____ _____ that are made of tubelike cells.

2 Nonvascular plants _____ vascular tissues to transport food and nutrients.

3 _____ _____ involves both male and female parts.

4 Mosses reproduce _____ in their first stage of reproduction.

5 When there is enough _____, the sperm cells move to the eggs and fertilize them.

C Write the meaning of each word and phrase from Word List in English.

1	繁殖	_____	13	孢子	_____
2	無種子的	_____	14	相像的	_____
3	維管束植物	_____	15	獨立的	_____
4	非維管束植物	_____	16	階段	_____
5	維管束組織	_____	17	無性地；無性生殖地	_____
6	管狀的	_____	18	孢子囊	_____
7	普遍的；常見的	_____	19	潮濕的	_____
8	葉脈	_____	20	無性生殖	_____
9	蕨類植物	_____	21	精子（細胞）	_____
10	茂盛生長	_____	22	卵子（細胞）	_____
11	蕨葉	_____	23	受精卵	_____
12	地下莖	_____	24	有性生殖	_____

15 How Do Plants Respond to Their Environments?

🎧 36

A Listen to the passage and fill in the blanks.

1. All living things have _____ that help them survive. Plants also respond to their _____ to survive, but they _____ _____ respond more slowly than animals do. Tropisms and other _____ to certain conditions help plants meet their needs.

2. A plant's response to an external _____ is called a tropism. There are several types of _____. One is _____. In phototropism, plants grow or bend _____ sunlight. This enables plants to get as much light as possible so that they may _____ photosynthesis. Another is _____. This is how plants respond to _____. Plants' roots respond to the stimulus of gravity, so they grow _____ into the soil _____ their stems and leaves grow up in the air. _____ is the response of plants to water. Plants—especially their roots— grow toward _____ _____ _____ water.

3. Tropisms are all _____ responses by plants. They may be _____ positive or negative. For instance, the roots of a plant that grow down in the _____ of gravity show positive gravitropism. Stems that grow away from the _____ _____ gravity show negative gravitropism.

4. Plants have also adapted to their environments _____ _____ _____. For instance, desert environments are very dry and get _____ water. So _____ and other desert plants have adapted to the _____. They can _____ long periods of time without water and can also _____ large amounts of water inside them when it rains. Also, some plants that _____ little sunlight have adapted by becoming _____. Plants like the Venus flytrap _____ themselves by _____ and eating small insects. In this way, they can get enough _____ to survive.

B Complete each sentence with the correct word. Change the form if necessary.

> phototropism   sustain   stimulus   respond to   hydrotropism

1 A plant's response to an external _____ is called a tropism.

2 In _____, plants grow or bend toward sunlight.

3 Plants' roots _____ _____ the stimulus of gravity, so they grow downward into the soil.

4 _____ is the response of plants to water.

5 Some plants can _____ themselves with little water or sunlight.

C Write the meaning of each word and phrase from Word List in English.

1 適應	_____	12 重力	_____
2 對……做出反應	_____	13 向下	_____
3 傾向	_____	14 而	_____
4 向性	_____	15 向水性	_____
5 反應	_____	16 水源	_____
6 外部的	_____	17 非自主性的	_____
7 刺激	_____	18 忍受	_____
8 向光性	_____	19 貯藏	_____
9 彎曲	_____	20 肉食性的	_____
10 朝向	_____	21 捕蠅草	_____
11 向地性	_____	22 供養	_____

16 Understanding Numbers

🎧 37

A Listen to the passage and fill in the blanks.

1. The numerals we use today are called _____ _____. They are the ten _____ 0, 1, 2, 3, 4, 5, 6, 7, 8, and 9. Arabic numerals are based on the _____ _____. But sometimes we _____ Roman numerals. _____ _____ were used by the Romans. These were actually not numbers but letters or symbols that were used to _____ numbers. Each letter represented a different _____ _____. The letters and numbers that they _____ were this:

I = 1	V = 5	X = 10	L = _____
C = 100	D = _____	M = _____	

2. To make larger numbers, there were two _____. If the same size or a smaller letter _____ _____ another letter, you add their _____ together. A letter cannot _____ more than 3 times. So II is 1+1, or 2. III is 1+1+1, or ____. VI is 5+1, or ____. If the smaller letter comes _____ before the larger letter, you _____ the smaller one from the larger one. So, IV is 5–1, or 4. IX is 10–1, or ____. XL is _____ ____, or 40. This was extremely _____ and made doing math problems very _____. Imagine trying to _____ CCXII and XXXVI together.

3. _____, we use Arabic numerals today. Solving math problems with Arabic numerals is _____ _____ than with Roman numerals.

4. Let's learn more about _____. Numbers can be positive or _____. We can show them on a _____ _____. Numbers to the right of ____ are positive. Numbers to the _____ of 0 are negative. The number 0 is _____ positive nor negative.

5. We call these numbers _____ _____ or integers. Numbers with _____, like 0.2, 3.14, and _____ are not whole numbers. Neither are fractions or _____ _____ such as $\frac{1}{2}$ and ____ $\frac{3}{4}$.

6. _____ that are farther to the right on the number line are _____ (+5>+3). Integers that are _____ to the left on the number line are less (-1>-100). A _____ _____ is always greater than a negative integer (1>-100).

7. Another way to divide numbers is to _____ them as even and odd numbers. _____ _____ are any numbers that end in 0, 2, 4, 6, or 8. ____ is an even number. So are 36 and ____. _____ _____ are any numbers that end in 1, 3, 5, 7, or 9. 11, 53, and _____ are all odd numbers.

B Complete each sentence with the correct word. Change the form if necessary.

> even number   easy   Arabic numeral   decimal   Roman numeral

1 The numerals we use today are called _____ _____.

2 _____ _____ were not numbers but symbols that were used to represent numbers.

3 Solving math problems with Arabic numerals is much _____ than with Roman numerals.

4 Numbers with _____, fractions, or mixed numbers are not whole numbers.

5 _____ _____ are any numbers that end in 0, 2, 4, 6, or 8.

C Write the meaning of each word and phrase from Word List in English.

1	阿拉伯數字	_____	15 正的	_____
2	數字	_____	16 負的	_____
3	十進制	_____	17 數線	_____
4	遇到	_____	18 既非……也非……	_____
5	羅馬數字	_____	19 整數	w_____
6	代表	_____	20 整數	i_____
7	數值	_____	21 小數	_____
8	規則	_____	22 分數	_____
9	重複	_____	23 帶分數	_____
10	減去	_____	24 正整數	_____
11	非常地；極端地	_____	25 負整數	_____
12	複雜的	_____	26 偶數	_____
13	想像	_____	27 奇數	_____
14	幸運地	_____	28 以……結尾	_____

🎧 38

A **Listen to the passage and fill in the blanks.**

1 _____ is the study of points, lines, and _____. It is also the study of the shapes and _____ that can be _____ using points, lines, and angles.

2 A polygon is a closed _____ _____ formed by three or more _____ _____. Polygons are named by the number of sides, angles, or _____ they have.

3 Polygons with three sides are called _____. We classify triangles according to the _____ of their sides and their angles.

4 Figures that have _____ the same size and shape are _____. Figures that have the same shape, but not the same size, are _____. The lengths of _____ sides of similar figures are _____.

5 Four-sided polygons are called _____. There are five special types of quadrilaterals: _____, rectangles, squares, rhombuses, and trapezoids.

6 A parallelogram has two pairs of _____ _____. The opposite sides and _____ angles are congruent.

7 A _____ is a parallelogram in which all the angles are _____ _____ and the opposite sides are the same length. A square has four _____ _____ and four right angles.

8 A _____ is a parallelogram with all _____ _____ congruent. It also has two _____ _____ _____ that run along its diagonals.

9 A _____ also has four sides, but it only has one _____ _____ parallel sides.

10 A polygon with five sides is a _____. One with six sides is a _____. A heptagon has seven sides while an _____ has eight. A _____ has nine sides, and a _____ has ten. In _____, a polygon can have an _____ number of sides. But all of the sides must _____ to form a closed figure.

B Complete each sentence with the correct word. Change the form if necessary.

> unlimited   line segment   congruent   proportional   quadrilateral

1 A polygon is a closed plane figure formed by three or more _____ _____.

2 Figures that have exactly the same size and shape are _____.

3 The sides of similar figures are _____ to one another.

4 Four-sided polygons are called _____.

5 In theory, a polygon can have an _____ number of sides.

C Write the meaning of each word and phrase from Word List in English.

1 幾何學 _____

2 作圖；畫 _____

3 多邊形 _____

4 封閉圖形 _____

5 平面圖形 _____

6 頂點 _____

7 等邊三角形 _____

8 等腰三角形 _____

9 不等邊三角形；不規則三角形 _____

10 全等的 _____

11 對應邊 _____

12 相似圖形 _____

13 成比例的 _____

14 四邊形 _____

15 平行四邊形 _____

16 菱形 _____

17 梯形 _____

18 平行的 _____

19 對稱軸 _____

20 對角線的 _____

21 五邊形 _____

22 六邊形 _____

23 七邊形 _____

24 八邊形 _____

25 九邊形 _____

26 十邊形 _____

27 理論上 _____

28 無限的 _____

18 The *Iliad* and the *Odyssey*

🎧 39

A Listen to the passage and fill in the blanks.

1 Around _____ years ago, there lived the greatest _____ in ancient
Greece. He was a man named _____. According to _____, Homer was a
blind poet. He told two of the _____ stories of all time, the *Iliad* and the *Odyssey*.
The *Iliad* and the *Odyssey* are long _____ _____ about great heroes, gods,
and _____ in ancient Greece. Homer was an _____ poet, so his poems
were _____ _____ later by people.

2 The *Iliad* tells about the _____ _____, a long war between the Greeks and the
people of Troy. Paris, a prince of Troy, _____ Helen, the wife of the _____
Menelaus and the most beautiful woman in the world. All of the Greek leaders joined
together and _____ Troy. There were many great _____. They included
Ajax, _____, and Agamemnon. But the greatest Greek _____ was
Achilles. He was _____ in battle and could not be defeated, except for on his
_____, his only weak spot. Meanwhile, the greatest hero _____ Troy was
Hector.

3 The Trojan War _____ for ten years. Troy eventually _____ because of a clever
plan by the Greeks that was _____ _____ Odysseus. The Greeks built a giant
_____ statue of a horse. They left it outside the walls of the city of Troy and
_____ _____ leave. The Trojans brought the _____ inside the city
because they believed it was an _____ to the gods. But there were Greek warriors
_____ in the Trojan Horse. That night, the Greek warriors _____ _____
of the horse, opened the gates, and _____ Troy at last.

4 The _____ tells about the return home of Odysseus. It took Odysseus ten years to
_____ home after the Trojan War. _____ _____ _____ home to Ithaca,
Odysseus had many difficult adventures. He was _____ killed by the one-eyed
_____ Polyphemus. He was also almost turned into a pig by the _____
Circe. He visited the _____, too. He lost his entire _____. However, thanks
to the gods — especially _____ — Odysseus returned home and was _____
_____ his faithful wife Penelope.

B Complete each sentence with the correct word. Change the form if necessary.

> write down   storyteller   wooden   Homer   Trojan War   Odyssey

1 There lived the greatest _____ in ancient Greece named _____.

2 The *Iliad* and the *Odyssey* were _____ _____ later by people.

3 The *Iliad* tells about the _____ _____, a long war between the Geeks and the Trojans.

4 The Greeks built a giant _____ statue of a horse, the Trojan Horse.

5 The _____ tells about the return home of Odysseus after the Trojan War.

C Write the meaning of each word and phrase from Word List in English.

1 講故事的人 _____

2 傳說 _____

3 盲的 _____

4 伊里亞德 _____

5 奧德賽 _____

6 史詩 _____

7 口述的 _____

8 被記載下來 _____

9 特洛伊戰爭 _____

10 綁架；劫持 _____

11 墨涅拉俄斯 _____

12 攻擊 _____

13 阿傑克斯 _____

14 奧德修斯 _____

15 阿卡曼農 _____

16 阿基里斯 _____

17 令人生畏的 _____

18 腳後跟 _____

19 弱點 _____

20 保衛 _____

21 赫克特 _____

22 由……設計 _____

23 假裝 _____

24 禮物；供品 _____

25 自……爬出 _____

26 在途中 _____

27 差點 _____

28 獨眼巨人 _____

29 女巫 _____

30 被……迎接 _____

🎧 40

A Listen to the passage and fill in the blanks.

1 When writers create _____, they use both literal and figurative language. _____ _____ says exactly what you mean. Much _____ uses literal language. However, many writers _____ figurative language as well. This makes their writing much more _____. It also gives their writing more _____. There are many different _____ for writers to use _____ language.

2 One way is to use _____ ____ _____. A figure of speech is an _____ that is not meant to be taken _____. These often create images in the _____ _____. Similes and metaphors are two of the most _____ figures of speech. Both are _____. However, _____ are direct comparisons while metaphors are _____ comparisons.

3 In addition, similes often use "as" or "like" to _____ two things. For instance, one simile is "Love is like a _____." Many similes _____ _____ animals. "He _____ like a lion" and "She was as _____ as a lamb" are two more similes. Metaphors are not ____ _____ ____ similes. _____ compare two unlike things that seem to have nothing ____ _____. And they do not use "like" or "____." "She is the _____ of my eye," "He is a _____," and "There is a sea of _____" are examples of metaphors.

4 Another common figure of speech is _____. This is the giving of human _____ to animals, plants, things, or ideas. "The moon is _____," "The walls have _____," and "Time waits for no one" are examples of personification.

5 Some writers like to use _____ in their works. This is using words that sound like the things that they _____. For instance, a snake might "_____," a bee might "_____," and a bell might go "ding dong."

B Complete each sentence with the correct word. Change the form if necessary.

> literally   literal language   onomatopoeia   metaphor   personification

1 _____ _____ says exactly what you mean.

2 A figure of speech is an expression that is not meant to be taken _____.

3 Similes and _____ are two of the most popular figures of speech.

4 _____ is the giving of human characteristics to animals, plants, things, or ideas.

5 _____ is using words that sound like the things that they describe.

C Write the meaning of each word and phrase from Word List in English.

1 文學；文學作品 _____

2 字面性語言 _____

3 比喻性語言 _____

4 使用 _____

5 富創造力的 _____

6 想像力 _____

7 修辭（手法）_____

8 照字面地 _____

9 讀者 _____

10 心 _____

11 明喻 _____

12 隱喻 _____

13 普遍的 _____

14 比喻；比較 _____

15 直接 _____

16 間接 _____

17 涉及；關於 _____

18 溫順的 _____

19 小羊 _____

20 像……一樣明顯 _____

21 共同的 _____

22 驟 _____

23 擬人法 _____

24 擬聲法 _____

20 Classical Art
Greek and Roman Art

🎧 41

A Listen to the passage and fill in the blanks.

☐1 In art history, Classical Art has been a very _____ period of art to many later eras. _____ _____ refers to art from ancient Greece and Rome. The ancient _____ and _____ created many wonderful _____ _____ _____, including pottery, sculptures, and buildings.

☐2 Classical Art _____ _____ simplicity and proportion. The ancient Greeks _____ the way. They considered balance and _____ to be the most important qualities in art. One of the easiest ways to understand Classical Art is to look at the _____ of this period.

☐3 When the ancient Greeks built buildings, they used _____ as supports and followed one of three classical orders: Doric, Ionic, and Corinthian. Most columns have a _____ at the bottom, a shaft in the middle, and a _____ at the top. The _____ _____ was the oldest and simplest in style and usually had no base. The _____ _____ had capitals decorated with spiral scrolls. And the _____ _____ had the most decorated and _____ capitals.

☐4 The Romans were _____ of Greek art and created copies of many Greek works. But they also introduced some new _____ from the Egyptians.

☐5 In Greece, the _____ of Apollo, the Temple of Hera, and the Parthenon are _____ of Classical architecture. In Rome, the _____ and the Pantheon are two examples. The buildings are all _____ and are fine examples of the classical _____ on balance and proportion.

☐6 The ancient Greeks and Romans also created many beautiful _____. They focused on the beauty of nature and the _____ of the human body. They _____ the human body as a _____ and harmonious form. Myron's *Discus Thrower* and *Apollo Belvedere* are _____ examples that show the beauty and proportion of the _____ _____.

B Complete each sentence with the correct word. Change the form if necessary.

> Classical Art   focus on   column   admirer   harmony

1 _____ _____ refers to art from ancient Greece and Rome.

2 Classical Art _____ _____ simplicity and proportion.

3 When the ancient Greeks built buildings, they used _____ as supports and followed one of three classical orders.

4 The Romans were _____ of Greek art and created copies of many Greek works.

5 The ancient Greek and Roman sculptors focused on the beauty of nature and the _____ of the human body.

C Write the meaning of each word and phrase from Word List in English.

1	古典藝術	_____	15	柱礎	_____
2	有影響的	_____	16	柱身	_____
3	之後的年代	_____	17	柱頭	_____
4	陶器	_____	18	以……裝飾	_____
5	雕刻品	_____	19	螺旋形的	_____
6	著重在	_____	20	渦卷形裝飾	_____
7	簡單；樸素	_____	21	精巧的；複雜的	_____
8	均衡；比例	_____	22	崇拜者	_____
9	建築物；建築風格	_____	23	元素	_____
10	圓柱	_____	24	羅馬競技場	_____
11	古典柱式	_____	25	對稱的	_____
12	多立克柱式	_____	26	優秀的；好的	_____
13	愛奧尼柱式	_____	27	強調	_____
14	科林斯柱式	_____	28	勻稱的	_____

21 Classical Music
The Western Musical Tradition

🎧 42

A Listen to the passage and fill in the blanks.

1. Throughout history, there have been many _____ _____ music. Among the most famous are the _____, Classical, and Romantic periods. The composers who lived during these periods wrote some of the greatest of all _____ _____.

2. The Baroque Period lasted from around _____ to _____. Two of its _____ composers were Johann Sebastian Bach and George Frederic Handel. Many new forms of music, such as _____, oratorios, and _____, were created in the Baroque Period. There was often an _____ on religious music. Both Bach and Handel are well _____ _____ their music with religious _____. Bach _____ *St. Matthew Passion*. Handel wrote *The* _____, which contains the *Hallelujah Chorus*. Baroque music was often _____ and difficult to play. It was also known for its _____. Handel's *Water Music* and *Royal Fireworks Music* are _____ pieces from that age.

3. The next great age was the _____ _____. It lasted from around 1750 to _____. Wolfgang Amadeus Mozart, Joseph Haydn, and Ludwig van _____ are the three greatest composers from this era. All three men were born in _____, Austria, so Vienna became the _____ _____ of this period. Classical music was both _____ and less complicated than Baroque. Unlike Baroque music, the _____ in a piece of Classical music often changed, and the pieces were _____ as well. Sonatas and _____ were popular then. Beethoven's *Ninth Symphony*, _____ *The Marriage of Figaro*, and _____ *Surprise Symphony* are some popular works from that period.

4. The Romantic Period lasted from around _____ to _____. The works then often expressed strong emotions, making them _____. Fantasy and imagination were key _____ for the composers when they were writing their music. More instruments were added to the _____ than were used _____ the Classical Period. Many works in this period, like _____ _____ Richard Wagner, were quite long. Among the famous composers of the _____ _____ were Franz Schubert, Robert Schumann, and Frederic _____.

B Complete each sentence with the correct word. Change the form if necessary.

> Baroque Period   emphasis   Classical music   Romantic Period   fantasy

1 Johann Bach and George Handel are two greatest composers from the
  _____ _____.

2 There was often an _____ on religious music in the Baroque Period.

3 _____ _____ was both lighter and less complicated than Baroque.

4 _____ and imagination were key aspects for the composers in the Romantic
  Period.

5 Among the famous composers of the _____ _____ were Schubert,
  Schumann, and Chopin.

C Write the meaning of each word and phrase from Word List in English.

1 巴洛克時期 _____

2 古典時期 _____

3 浪漫時期 _____

4 神劇 _____

5 熱情；激情 _____

6 以……著名 _____

7 宗教主題 _____

8 複雜的 _____

9 活潑；輕快 _____

10 代表性的 _____

11 誕生於 _____

12 焦點 _____

13 曲調 _____

14 第九號交響曲 _____

15 費加洛婚禮 _____

16 驚愕交響曲 _____

17 情感 _____

18 熱情的；激昂的 _____

19 幻想 _____

20 主要層面 _____

Answer Key

Daily Test 01
1 landforms   2 stretches   3 rainfall
4 metropolitan   5 dominated

Daily Test 02
1 streamed into   2 As a result
3 ethnic group   4 discrimination   5 races

Daily Test 03
1 free market   2 free-enterprise
3 supply   4 scarce   5 entrepreneur

Daily Test 04
1 ancestors   2 civilizations   3 adapted
4 wandered   5 archaeologist

Daily Test 05
1 competed to   2 sponsor   3 round
4 circumnavigation   5 Age of Exploration

Daily Test 06
1 in search of   2 Aztec Empire
3 Inca Empire   4 Smallpox   5 enslaved

Daily Test 07
1 permanent, Quebec   2 settlement
3 Puritans   4 separate   5 the east coast

Daily Test 08
1 pay off   2 boycotting   3 representatives
4 Declaration of Independence   5 colonies

Daily Test 09
1 kingdoms   2 Protista   3 feed on
4 microscopic   5 Animalia

Daily Test 10
1 levels, genus   2 depends on   3 specific
4 precise   5 determines

Daily Test 11
1 parts, functions   2 prevent
3 responsible for   4 Chloroplasts
5 oxygen

Daily Test 12
1 female   2 pollinating   3 transferred
4 pollen tube   5 fertilized

Daily Test 13
1 seed plants   2 based on   3 division
4 female cones   5 dominant

Daily Test 14
1 vascular tissues   2 lack
3 Sexual reproduction   4 asexually
5 moisture

Daily Test 15
1 stimulus   2 phototropism
3 respond to   4 Hydrotropism
5 sustain

Daily Test 16
1 Arabic numerals   2 Roman numerals
3 easier   4 decimals   5 Even numbers

Daily Test 17
1 line segments   2 congruent
3 proportional   4 quadrilaterals
5 unlimited

Daily Test 18
1 storyteller, Homer   2 written down
3 Trojan War   4 wooden   5 *Odyssey*

Daily Test 19
1 Literal language   2 literally
3 metaphors   4 Personification
5 Onomatopoeia

Daily Test 20
1 Classical Art   2 focuses on   3 columns
4 admirers   5 harmony

Daily Test 21
1 Baroque Period   2 emphasis
3 Classical music   4 Fantasy
5 Romantic Period

1

- **Social Studies**
- **History and Geography**

Visual Preview What are some features of the different regions in the United States?

New York City is a large metropolitan area with millions of people.

Farms cover huge amounts of land all throughout the American Midwest.

The Rocky Mountains rise high above the land in the Mountain States.

Vocabulary Preview Write the correct word and the meaning in Chinese next to its meaning.

| dominate | diverse | fertile | arid | cash crop |

1 _____ : a crop that is grown to be sold for money

2 _____ : to overlook from a superior elevation or command because of superior height or position

3 _____ : rich; productive

4 _____ : very dry; having very little rain or water

5 _____ : varied; having many different types or variations

The Regions of the United States

🎧 01

▲ Washington, D.C., the nation's capital

The United States can be divided into five geographic regions. Each region has its own **physical environment**, such as **landforms** and climate. These features set each region apart from the other ones.

The Northeast region includes 11 states and the nation's capital, Washington, D.C. (District of Columbia). The Atlantic Coastal Plain and mountain ranges are the Northeast's major landforms. The Northeast is often divided into two subregions: New England and the Middle Atlantic States.

In American history, many of the first settlers from Europe settled in the Northeast. New England is known for the early settlements by the Pilgrims and Puritans. The Middle Atlantic has some of the most densely populated areas and largest urban areas in the U.S., including New York City, Washington, D.C., and Philadelphia.

The Southeast includes 12 states. The Mississippi River flows through the western part of the region. A warm climate and a long growing season in the Southeast help farmers grow many different kinds of **cash crops**. Tobacco and cotton were some of the first cash crops for early plantation owners. Peaches in Georgia and oranges in sunny Florida are two important cash crops for modern Southeast farmers.

▲ cash crop

The Midwest is a region of plains and **prairies**. The Great Plains and the Central Plains are known for their rich fields of corn, soybeans, and wheat that **stretch** as far as the eye can see. The Mississippi River begins there, and four of the Great Lakes are in the Midwest. Its flat land and **fertile croplands** make this region a center for agriculture. People often call the Midwest "the Breadbasket of the United States."

▲ prairie

The Southwest includes Arizona, New Mexico, Texas, and Oklahoma. The region has many **arid** and range areas, so it contains several deserts. There are also numerous plateaus, canyons, mesas, and buttes. The Grand Canyon, one of the best-known landforms in the U.S., is located in the Southwest.

▲ Grand Canyon

Finally, the West includes California, Nevada, Oregon, Washington, and the Mountain States. Alaska and Hawaii are in the western region, but they are separate from the continental United States. The region is a **diverse** area with many different environments. The Northwest is known for its long coastlines along the Pacific Ocean while the Southwest is dry and contains many deserts. Much of the Mountain States is **dominated** by the Rocky Mountains.

▲ the rocky coastline of California

▲ Rocky Mountains

Quick Check Check T (True) or F (False).

1 There are two smaller regions found within the Northeast.   T F
2 The breadbasket of the United States is the Southeast.   T F
3 The Grand Canyon is located in the Mountain States.   T F

1 **What is the passage mainly about?**

    a. Where each region in the United States is.

    b. What the name of each region in the U.S. is.

    c. How each region in the U.S. is different from the others.

2 **Tobacco, cotton, and peaches are important cash crops in the** _____.

    a. Northeast   **b.** Southwest   **c.** Southeast

3 **Why do people call the Midwest "the Breadbasket of the United States"?**

    a. It is an important farming center in the country.

    b. The people living there enjoy many kinds of bread.

    c. Much of the land in the Midwest is flat.

4 **What does densely mean?**

    a. Partially.   **b.** Heavily.   **c.** Actively.

5 **Complete the sentences.**

    a. There are many large _____ areas in the Northeast.

    b. Farmers in the _____ grow corn, soybeans, and wheat.

    c. Neither Alaska nor _____ borders any other states in the U.S.

6 **Complete the outline.**

American Regions
• a_____ = has 11 states plus Washington, D.C.
• Southeast = has 12 states
• Midwest = includes many states with plains and prairies
• b_____ = Arizona, New Mexico, Texas, and Oklahoma
• West = California, Nevada, Oregon, Washington, and the c_____ _____

American Landforms
• Coastal areas = land next to water
• Urban areas = densely d_____ areas like New York City and Boston
• Freshwater areas = the Mississippi and the Great Lakes areas
• Croplands = land with farms on them
• Arid and e_____ areas = deserts

Complete each sentence. Change the form if necessary.

physical environment   arid   stretch   landform   dominate

1 The _____ of a region includes its landforms and climate.

2 Plains and prairies are major _____ in the Midwest.

3 _____ regions get very little rainfall all throughout the year.

4 The Midwest region is _____ by croplands.

5 The continental United States _____ from Canada to Mexico.

Unit 02 The United States

Visual Preview Why is the United States sometimes called a "nation of diversity"?

People from many different countries live together in the United States.

Immigration there has been ongoing since Columbus discovered America in 1492.

There was social discrimination against some ethnic groups, but now people are treated fairly.

Vocabulary Preview Write the correct word and the meaning in Chinese next to its meaning.

immigrant   stream   concentrate   ethnic group   discrimination

1 _____ : people who share the same customs, language, and history

2 _____ : to bring or come together in a large number or amount

3 _____ : a person who leaves his or her country to move to another one

4 _____ : treating someone poorly because of that person's race, gender, or religion

5 _____ : to move in large numbers in a continuous flow

A Nation of Diversity

The United States is sometimes called a nation of **immigrants**. People from many different countries and races live there. It took centuries for the United States to become a **multicultural** society. And the country's people did not come from all over the world at the same time. In fact, immigration to America happened in various stages.

After Christopher Columbus discovered America in 1492, many Europeans started to move to America. The first Europeans to come to America were English, Germans, Irish, Dutch, and French. Many Africans started coming as well. But they were slaves, so they were brought to America against their will.

Then, between 1880 and 1924, a second wave of immigrants poured into the United States. Many of these **newcomers** came from Southern and Eastern European countries, including Italy, Poland, and Russia. Since the late

◀ Lady Liberty, a symbol of freedom to immigrants

1800s, Asian immigrants—people from China, Japan, Korea, and other countries—have **streamed** into the western United States.

While the first immigrants often spread out to rural areas, later immigrants **concentrated** in the cities. For instance, New York and Boston were homes to Italian and Jewish immigrants, the largest **ethnic groups** in the second wave of immigrants. Chicago was home to a mixture of many races and nationalities.

▲ 19th century immigrants

Today, the United States has citizens from almost every country. But not all nationalities have always gotten along with each other. Immigrants sometimes encountered **discrimination**. Early immigrants, such as English settlers, Irish, and Germans, shared much with English culture. However, later immigrants were very different. They spoke different languages and had different religions and customs. Some people who were already well settled disliked more poor newcomers arriving. **As a result**, social discrimination against blacks, Jews, Asians, and other ethnic groups continued into the 1900s.

▲ ethnic group

However, the U.S. government passed laws to end discrimination in the 1960s. Now, all people are treated **fairly** no matter what race they are. So, most Americans live together **in harmony**.

▲ The U.S. is a multicultural society.

Quick Check Check T (True) or F (False).

1 The first Africans to come to America were mostly slaves. ☐T ☐F
2 Asians began to come to the United States in the late 1800s. ☐T ☐F
3 People who were already well settled welcomed newcomers. ☐T ☐F

1 What is the main idea of the passage?
a. There are more Europeans than Asians in the United States.
b. Immigrants from all over the world came to the United States.
c. There was once a lot of racial discrimination in the United States.

2 After Columbus discovered America, most of the people who went there were _____.
a. Africans   b. Asians   c. Europeans

3 Where did many Italian immigrants to the United States live?
a. New York.   b. Chicago.   c. Los Angeles.

4 What does encountered mean?
a. Passed.   b. Disliked.   c. Experienced.

5 According to the passage, which statement is true?
a. There was only one stage of immigration to the United States.
b. Many immigrants came to the United States between 1880 and 1924.
c. Jews and Asians suffered no social discrimination in the United States.

6 Complete the outline.

Immigration

First Wave
• Came after Christopher Columbus discovered America
• Were mostly from ᵃ_____
• Were some ᵇ_____ slaves

Second Wave
• Was from 1880 to 1924
• Came from Southern and ᶜ_____ Europe
• Came from Asian countries

Discrimination

Early Immigrants
• Shared much with English culture so had few problems

Later Immigrants
• Had different languages, ᵈ_____, and cultures
• There was social discrimination against blacks, Jews, and ᵉ_____.
• Laws were passed to end discrimination in the 1960s.

Vocabulary Review   Complete each sentence. Change the form if necessary.

stream into	as a result	fairly	concentrate in	in harmony

1 _____ _____ _____ of the new laws, discrimination is now illegal.

2 All people should be treated _____ no matter where they are from.

3 It is important for people to live _____ _____ with one another.

4 Immigrants _____ _____ the vast empty land in the United States in the 1800s.

5 Many Asians are _____ _____ the Western United States in places such as California.

Visual Preview What is a free market economy?

People choose what to produce and what to buy without government interference.

People choose how they earn and spend their money.

The prices of goods and services depend on the law of supply and demand.

Vocabulary Preview Write the correct word and the meaning in Chinese next to its meaning.

entrepreneur	free market	interference	opportunity cost	distribute

1 _____ : an economy in which people, not the government, decide what to make, buy, and sell

2 _____ : the value of the second best choice; an item a person does not purchase

3 _____ : a person who starts his or her own business

4 _____ : to give or deliver (something) to people; to deliver (something) to a store or business

5 _____ : the process of deliberately becoming involved in a situation and trying to influence the way that it develops

From Farming to Technology

🎧 03

An economy is the way that goods and services are produced and **distributed**. The economy of a country includes the activities of all producers and consumers within that country. A strong economy produces many goods and services.

Today, the gross domestic product (GDP) of the United States is the highest of any country in the world. The GDP is the total amount of goods and services produced within a country in a year. So having the highest GDP in the world means that the U.S. has the largest economy in the world.

The early American economy was **based on** farming. The majority of colonists who came to America from Europe in the 1600s and 1700s were

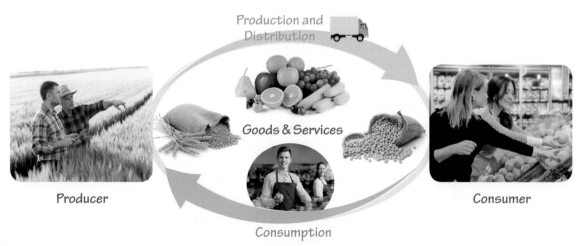

Production and Distribution

Goods & Services

Producer

Consumption

Consumer

farmers. Later, the manufacturing and service industries made up the largest parts of the economy. Today, the finance and technology industries are the fastest-growing parts of the economy.

▲ **manufacturing industry**

In the United States, people and companies are part of a **free market** economy. In a free market, people choose what to produce and what to buy. Farmers decide what crops to plant. Factory owners decide what products to manufacture. Storeowners decide what kinds of products to sell. And consumers consider **opportunity cost** when they make decisions about buying these goods and services. People can choose how they earn and spend their money without government **interference**. The American economy is also based on the **free-enterprise** system. This means that people can own and run their own businesses. People who start and run their own businesses are called **entrepreneurs**.

▲ **technology**

▲ **distribution**

In most cases, people who sell goods or services decide on their prices according to the law of **supply** and **demand**.

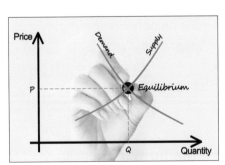
▲ **the law of supply and demand**

If the supply is large yet demand is low, the price usually goes down. If the supply is **scarce** or small yet demand is high, then the price often rises.

▲ **entrepreneur**

Quick Check Check T (True) or F (False).

1   The United States has the second highest GDP in the world.   ☐ T ☐ F

2   Farming was the basis of the early American economy.   ☐ T ☐ F

3   In a free market, the government makes most economic decisions.   ☐ T ☐ F

1   **What is the passage mainly about?**
   a. The history of the American economy.
   b. Why the U.S. economy is so strong.
   c. The American economic system.

2   **Most early American colonists were _____ .**
   a. farmers   **b.** businessmen   **c.** factory owners

3   **What usually happens when the supply of a product is high but the demand is low?**
   a. The price of the product goes up.   **b.** The price of the product goes down.
   c. The price of the product stays the same.

4   **What does consumers mean?**
   a. Buyers.   **b.** Manufacturers.   **c.** Owners.

5   **Answer the questions.**
   a. What does GDP stand for? _____
   b. What are some of the fastest-growing parts of the U.S. economy today?

   _____

   c. What is the free-enterprise system? _____

6   **Complete the outline.**

The American Economy

Early Economy
• Was based on ^{a}_____

Changes to the Economy
• Manufacturing and service industries became important.
• ^{b}_____ and technology industries are the fastest-growing parts.

Free Market Economy
• People can choose what to produce and buy.

Economic Terms

• ^{c}_____ = gross domestic product
• Opportunity cost → Consumers make decisions on what to buy.
• Entrepreneur = a person who starts and runs his or her own ^{d}_____
• Supply = the amount of a product
• ^{e}_____ = how much people want a product

Complete each sentence. Change the form if necessary.

distribute	based on	interference	free-enterprise	scarce

1   Companies must _____ their products to markets where they can be sold.

2   Most businessmen dislike any _____ from the government.

3   When some products are _____ , their prices increase.

4   The American economy was once _____ _____ agriculture.

5   The _____ system gives people choices in how they make money.

How did early Native Americans adapt to their environment?

Hunter-gatherers followed animals and crossed a land bridge to America.

Some tribes hunted buffaloes and lived in teepees.

Some tribes adapted to the harsh, arid environment in the desert.

Write the correct word and the meaning in Chinese next to its meaning.

hunter-gatherer	archaeologist	alliance	wander	herd

1 _____ : a person who studies past human civilizations

2 _____ : a person who hunts animals and collects vegetation for food

3 _____ : to move around or go to different places usually without having a particular purpose or direction

4 _____ : an agreement of friendship between two or more people or groups

5 _____ : a group of animals that live or are kept together

The Native People of North America

🎧 04

▲ hunter-gatherer

▲ buffalo hunting

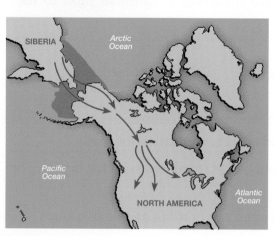

◄ land bridge

Around 15,000 years ago, the first native people arrived in the Americas. Many **archaeologists** believe they crossed a land bridge from Asia.

During the Ice Age, there was narrow strip of land that connected Asia and North America. From Asia, big **herds** of animals moved across that land bridge looking for food, and the first people followed the animals that supplied their food. During their hunting trips, they also gathered wild berries, nuts, and fruits for food. That is why we call them **hunter-gatherers**.

As the years passed, more and more people came across the land bridge, and they spread all over the Americas. These people were the **ancestors** of the Native Americans. Over time, early Native Americans began to grow food and to build homes. They **settled in** various places and built **civilizations**.

Many Native American **tribes** adapted to their environments. Cultures developed according to the climate and the natural resources of the tribes' surroundings. This caused each tribe to live differently from the others.

In the Great Plains area of North America, there were tribes like the Sioux and Lakota. They hunted buffaloes for food and **wandered** the land. They lived in teepees, cone-shaped tents that they could transport from place to place.

In the Southwest, there were tribes such as the Pueblo and Navajo. They adapted to the harsh, arid environment in the desert. The Pueblo farmed in the desert using a method called dry farming. They built homes, called pueblos, out of adobe. Adobe protected their homes from extreme heat and cold.

In the West, the Inuit in Alaska hunted whales for food and clothing. The Tlingit were skilled craft workers. They used wood to make totem poles, canoes, and **crafts**.

And in the East, the Iroquois built longhouses using materials from the forests. Some tribes even formed an **alliance** called the Iroquois Confederacy. They were among the first Native Americans to deal with European colonists when they arrived in North America.

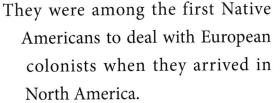
▲ crafts

▲ the Sioux   teepee

▲ the Tlingit   totem pole

▲ the Iroquois   longhouse

▲ the Pueblo   pueblo

Quick Check Check T (True) or F (False).

1 The first people in the Americas crossed a land bridge from Africa.   ☐ T ☐ F
2 The Sioux and Lakota lived in teepees.   ☐ T ☐ F
3 Some Native American tribes hunted whales.   ☐ T ☐ F

1 **What is the passage mainly about?**
   a. When the first people arrived and spread in the Americas.
   b. How the lives of early people were different from the lives of people today.
   c. How early people came to the Americas and adapted to their environments.

2 **The _____ tribe made use of dry farming.**
   a. Iroquois   **b.** Lakota   **c.** Pueblo

3 **How did the first tribes that entered the Americas get their food?**
   a. By hunting and gathering.   **b.** By farming the land.   **c.** By killing whales.

4 **What does transport mean?**
   a. Build.   **b.** Put up.   **c.** Move.

5 **Complete the sentences.**
   a. The first people in the Americas followed herds of _____ across a land bridge.
   b. The Pueblo built their homes out of _____.
   c. The _____ tribe lived in longhouses and formed the Iroquois Confederacy.

6 **Complete the outline.**

How the First People Came to the Americas
• Crossed a ᵃ_____ from Asia about 15,000 years ago
• Were following herds of animals
• Were ᵇ_____
• Spread out over the Americas
• Were the ancestors of Native Americans

The Lives of Native Tribes
• Sioux and Lakota = lived in teepees and hunted ᶜ_____ on the Great Plains
• Pueblo and Navajo = lived in the desert and used dry farming
• Inuit = hunted whales
• ᵈ_____ = were skilled crafts workers
• Iroquois = made longhouses and founded the Iroquois ᵉ_____

Complete each sentence. Change the form if necessary.

civilization   ancestor   settle in   herd   wander

1 There were once many _____ of buffalo in the American West.

2 The Native Americans had their own _____.

3 The _____ of the Native Americans were the people who crossed the land bridge.

4 In the past, some tribes _____ the land in search of food.

5 The Pueblo _____ the harsh, arid desert.

The European Exploration of Asia and the Americas

Why did the Europeans sail around the world during the Age of Exploration?

The Europeans wanted to trade for spices, gold, and silk in Asia.

The Europeans competed to find water routes to Asia.

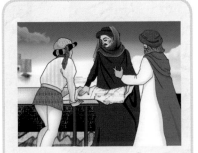

People like Prince Henry the Navigator sponsored many expeditions.

Write the correct word and the meaning in Chinese next to its meaning.

> caravel   sponsor   expedition   mission   circumnavigation

1 _____ : to provide funds for (a project or activity or the person carrying it out)

2 _____ : a fast sailing ship built by the Portuguese during the Age of Exploration

3 _____ : a long and carefully organized journey with a specific purpose

4 _____ : the act of traveling completely around the world

5 _____ : a task or job that someone is given to do

The Age of Exploration

🎧 05

▲ **Prince Henry the Navigator**

▲ **Bartolomeu Dias**

In the fifteenth century, many European countries, such as Portugal, Spain, France, and England, traded for goods from Asia. Gold, silk, and **spices** from India and China were in great demand in Europe. Europeans were **willing to** pay high prices for Asia's goods. However, it took a very long time for merchants to travel to Asia by land. So the Europeans began to search for another route to Asia.

The Europeans competed to find sea routes to Asia. Portugal led the way. The Portuguese developed a new ship, called the **caravel**, which could sail farther and faster than other ships. In 1418, Prince Henry the Navigator, a Portuguese prince, began sending **expeditions** to explore the western coast of Africa. Slowly, but **steadily**, the Portuguese sailed farther and farther south. Finally, in 1487, the Portuguese captain Bartolomeu Dias became the first European to **round**

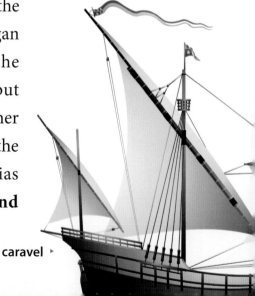

caravel ▶

26

the southern tip of Africa, the Cape of Good Hope. But he did not enter the Indian Ocean. Around ten years later, Vasco da Gama sailed all the way from Portugal to India. The Europeans had discovered a waterway to Asia.

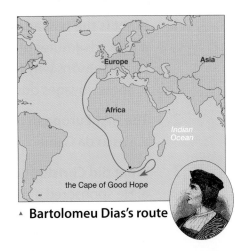

▲ **Bartolomeu Dias's route**

The Portuguese sailed to Asia by going around Africa. But Christopher Columbus, an Italian, believed he could reach Asia by sailing west across the Atlantic Ocean. He convinced Ferdinand and Isabella, the king and queen of Spain, to **sponsor** a three-ship **mission**. With his ships the *Pinta*, *Niña*, and *Santa María*, he **set sail** in 1492. After several weeks, his crew sighted land. It was not India though; it was the New World. Columbus had discovered North and South America.

In 1519, an expedition led by Ferdinand Magellan set sail from Spain. Magellan was killed in the Philippines, but his crew achieved the first **circumnavigation** of the world in 1522. Soon afterward, the French, Dutch, and English entered the race of global **exploration**, too.

▲ **Columbus's discovery of the New World**

The Europeans' sea explorations to reach Asia during the fifteenth and sixteenth centuries changed the world forever. We call this time "the Age of Exploration" or "the Age of Discovery."

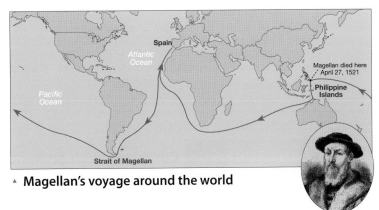

▲ **Magellan's voyage around the world**

Quick Check Check T (True) or F (False).

1 Prince Henry the Navigator sailed to the Cape of Good Hope. T F
2 Vasco da Gama led an expedition with the ships *Pinta*, *Niña*, and *Santa María*. T F
3 Ferdinand Magellan's crew was the first to circumnavigate the world. T F

1   **What is the passage mainly about?**
   a. The adventures of Prince Henry the Navigator.
   b. The reasons why the Europeans went to Asia.
   c. Some voyages during the Age of Exploration.

2   **The first European to sail to India was _____.**
   a. Vasco da Gama   **b.** Christopher Columbus   **c.** Bartolomeu Dias

3   **What did Christopher Columbus do?**
   a. He sponsored a trip around the Americas.
   b. He discovered the Americas.
   c. He sailed across the Atlantic Ocean to India.

4   **What does route mean?**
   a. Trip.   **b.** Map.   **c.** Path.

5   **According to the passage, which statement is NOT true?**
   a. It took a long time to travel from Europe to Asia.
   b. Ferdinand Magellan was the first European to sail to Asia.
   c. Bartolomeu Dias was the first European to reach the Cape of Good Hope.

6   **Complete the outline.**

Reasons for Sailing
• Gold, silk, and spices from Asia were in great ^{a}_____.   • Traveling to Asia by ^{b}_____ took a long time.   • ^{c}_____ let the Europeans sail very quickly on the oceans.

European Explorers
• Bartolomeu Dias = first European to round the Cape of ^{d}_____ _____   • Vasco da Gama = first European to sail to ^{e}_____   • Christopher Columbus = discovered America   • Ferdinand Magellan = His crew was the first to circumnavigate the world.

Complete each sentence. Change the form if necessary.

willing to   set sail   steadily   round   sponsor

1   The Europeans' knowledge of the world _____ increased during the Age of Exploration.

2   Most explorers needed someone to _____ their expeditions with money.

3   When did the expedition led by Ferdinand Magellan _____ _____ from Spain?

4   Many crew members were _____ ____ travel around the world to try to become rich.

5   It took many trips before the Portuguese could _____ the southern tip of Africa.

Visual Preview What happened after the Spanish conquistadors arrived in the New World?

The Aztec Empire in Central America was defeated by Hernando Cortés.

The Inca Empire in South America was destroyed by Francisco Pizarro.

The Spanish enslaved Native Americans and took much treasure from the natives.

Vocabulary Preview Write the correct word and the meaning in Chinese next to its meaning.

| conquistador | colony | claim | smallpox | immunity |

1 _____ : to say that something is yours, especially as a right

2 _____ : a serious disease in which your skin becomes covered in spots that can leave permanent marks

3 _____ : a Spanish conqueror

4 _____ : resistance to disease

5 _____ : an area ruled by the government of a faraway country

The Spanish Conquerors in the Americas

▲ Hernando Cortés with the Aztec emperor

▲ Francisco Pizarro

▲ two major Native American empires

After Columbus's discovery of America, more and more **Spaniards** came to the New World. Most came in search of gold, silver, and other treasures. They **proceeded to** make Spain the richest country in Europe. There were natives already in the Americas, of course, but the Spaniards ignored the rights of the local people.

In the sixteenth century, there were two major empires in Central and South America. One was the Aztec Empire in the land in modern-day Mexico. And the Inca Empire was in the South American land that is Peru today. Both the Aztecs and the Incas had a lot of gold and other riches that the Spaniards wanted.

30

In order to establish **colonies** in South America, Spain needed to conquer the Aztecs first. In 1519, Hernando Cortés sailed to Mexico with about 550 **conquistadors**. After just a few years, in 1521, the Spanish **captured** the Aztec capital Tenochtitlan and ended the Aztec Empire. A decade later, in 1532, another Spanish conquistador, Francisco Pizarro, conquered the Inca Empire. Pizarro led an expedition with only 185 men and 37 horses.

The Aztecs were fierce warriors, and the Incas were strong people, too. And the Spaniards had many fewer soldiers. So why did the Spanish win? They had much stronger weapons like guns, cannons, and metal armor. They rode horses, too, which the Native Americans had never seen before. The Spanish also had one more **deadly** weapon: disease. The Spanish arrived in the New World with horrible diseases like **smallpox**. The Native Americans had no **immunity** to these diseases, so thousands of them died. As a result, the Spanish easily defeated most Native American tribes. Then, they enslaved the natives and took their treasures. Spain also **claimed** a lot of land in North and South America and **set up** colonies.

▲ **Spanish conquistadors attacking the Aztecs**

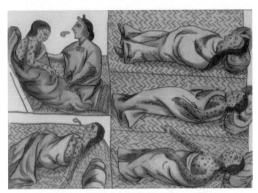

▲ **Native Americans dying of smallpox**

▲ **Native Americans enslaved by the Spanish**

Quick Check Check T (True) or F (False).

1   The Spanish conquered the Aztec and the Inca Empires.   T   F
2   The capital of the Inca Empire was Tenochtitlan.   T   F
3   The Native Americans rode on horses when they fought the Spaniards.   T   F

1 **What is the passage mainly about?**
a. How the Aztec Empire was defeated.
b. Who Hernando Cortés and Francisco Pizarro were.
c. What happened when the Spanish arrived in the Americas.

2 **Francisco Pizarro conquered the Inca Empire in** _____.
a. 1519   b. 1521   c. 1532

3 **Why did diseases like smallpox kill so many Native Americans?**
a. They had no immunity to the diseases.
b. They lacked medicines to treat the diseases.
c. Their doctors were not very good.

4 **What does fierce mean?**
a. Angry.   b. Outstanding.   c. Violent.

5 **Answer the questions.**
a. Why did many Spaniards go to the New World? _____
b. What were the two major Native American empires in Central and South America?

_____

c. How many men did Francisco Pizarro have with him? _____

6 **Complete the outline.**

Defeating the Natives

Aztec Empire
• Hernando Cortés had 550 conquistadors.
• Captured the Aztec ᵃ_____ Tenochtitlan in 1521

Inca Empire
• Francisco Pizarro had 185 men and 37 ᵇ_____.
• Conquered the Incas in 1532

How the Spanish Won

• Had much stronger ᶜ_____ like guns, cannons, and metal armor
• Rode ᵈ_____, which the Native Americans did not have
• ᵉ_____ and other diseases killed many natives.

Complete each sentence. Change the form if necessary.

proceed to	claim	smallpox	deadly	set up

1 The cannons and guns of the Spaniards were _____ to the Aztecs.

2 _____ and other diseases killed large numbers of Native Americans.

3 Cortés _____ _____ his own government to rule the Aztecs.

4 The Spanish _____ _____ seize large amounts of gold once they arrived in the Americas.

5 The Spanish _____ much land in the Americas for themselves.

07 Colonial America

What were the first French and English colonies in North America?

CANADA

St. Lawrence River

Quebec●

Samuel de Champlain built a permanent French settlement in Quebec in 1608.

Colonists at Jamestown, the first permanent English colony, had trouble during the early years.

The Pilgrims and Puritans settled in Massachusetts.

Vocabulary Preview Write the correct word and the meaning in Chinese next to its meaning.

| colonize | permanent | settlement | Puritans | prosper |

1 _____ : a deeply religious group of Christians who came from England

2 _____ : forever; lasting for a very long time

3 _____ : a place where settlers live

4 _____ : to take control of another country by going to live there or by sending people to live there

5 _____ : to become strong and flourishing

The First French and English Colonies

🎧 07

▲ Sieur de La Salle

▲ Jacques Cartier

While the Spanish focused on Central and South America, people from other European countries explored and **colonized** North America. On the east coast, the two most important countries were France and England.

The French mostly explored the area that is Canada today. In 1534, Jacques Cartier sailed down the St. Lawrence River. Other French explorers, such as Sieur de La Salle, explored the **interior** of North America. La Salle discovered the Mississippi River and **claimed** it for France. In 1608, Samuel de Champlain built a **permanent** French **settlement** in present-day Quebec.

The English mostly settled in the eastern part of the continent along the Atlantic Ocean. The first permanent English settlement was **founded** at Jamestown, Virginia,

◂ the first French settlement by Samuel de Champlain

34

in 1607. The **settlers** came there to seek their fortune. They wanted to get rich. But there was no gold, and many settlers died of hunger and disease. However, thanks to leaders like John Smith, who was saved by Pocahontas, the daughter of an Indian chief, Jamestown grew bigger and **prospered**.

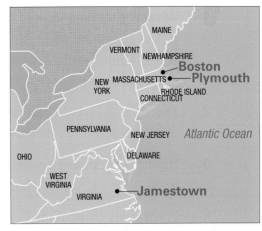

▲ the first English settlements

In 1620, another important English settlement was founded in present-day Massachusetts. It was started by the Pilgrims. They sailed on the *Mayflower* and landed in Plymouth, Massachusetts. They left England because of their religious beliefs.

▲ **Pocahontas saving John Smith's life**

Some other English colonists followed the Pilgrims. They were the **Puritans**. Like the Pilgrims, the Puritans were a deeply religious group of Christians. The Puritans settled in the area of present-day Boston, Massachusetts.

▲ **religious Puritans**

Over the next century, many more people moved from Europe to America. Most came from England, but some also came from France, Holland, and other countries. **Eventually**, they founded thirteen separate colonies. Every colony was on the east coast of the Atlantic. Later, these thirteen colonies would become the first states of the United States.

▲ **Pilgrims**

Quick Check Check T (True) or F (False).

1 The English were the first Europeans to see the Mississippi River.   T   F

2 France and England founded colonies on the east coast of North America.   T   F

3 The Puritans sailed to America on the *Mayflower*.   T   F

1 What is the main idea of the passage?
   a. There were more English than French in North America.
   b. The French mostly explored the area that is Canada today.
   c. Many people from England and France settled in North America.

2 The _____ landed in Plymouth, Massachusetts.
   a. Pilgrims   **b.** Puritans   **c.** Quakers

3 How many colonies were there when the United States became a country?
   a. 10.   **b.** 13.   **c.** 57.

4 What does chief mean?
   a. Leader.   **b.** Settler.   **c.** Tribe.

5 Complete the sentences.
   a. The French explorer _____ _____ sailed down the St. Lawrence River.
   b. The _____ was the name of the Pilgrim's ship.
   c. The Puritans moved to the area around _____, Massachusetts.

6 Complete the outline.

French Explorations
• Jacques Cartier = sailed down the   a_____ _____ River in 1534   • Sieur de La Salle = discovered the Mississippi River and explored the interior of America   • Samuel de Champlain = built a settlement in b_____ in 1608

English Explorations
• c_____, Virginia = first permanent English settlement in America in 1607   • Pilgrims = sailed on the *Mayflower* to Plymouth, d_____, in 1620   • Puritans = deeply e_____ Christians who founded a settlement near Boston, Massachusetts

Complete each sentence. Change the form if necessary.

colonize   eventually   settler   prosper   found

1   Many colonies were _____ by both the English and the French.

2   Some early _____ became friends with the Native Americans.

3   The English often _____ land next to the Atlantic Ocean.

4   It took many years before Jamestown began to _____ .

5   The English colonies _____ became very successful.

08 The Declaration of Independence

Visual Preview What caused the colonists to want independence from England?

British soldiers killed five American citizens at the Boston Massacre in 1770.

The colonists protested the taxes that raised money to pay the debt from the Seven Years' War.

Americans wanted to be represented in Parliament, but King George III refused.

Vocabulary Preview Write the correct word and the meaning in Chinese next to its meaning.

taxation   surrender   Parliament   minuteman   boycott

1 _____ : the system of charging taxes; the money collected from taxes

2 _____ : to refuse to buy, use, or participate in (something) as a way of protesting

3 _____ : American soldiers ready to fight "at a minute's notice"

4 _____ : to say officially that you have been defeated and will stop fighting

5 _____ : the English legislature

The American Revolution

🎧 08

▲ Seven Years' War

▲ King George III

▲ a tri-cornered hat, a symbolic hat during the American Revolution

In the 1760s, there were thirteen English colonies in America. A colony is an area ruled by the government of another country. The thirteen colonies in America were ruled by the king of England.

Meanwhile, from 1756 to 1763, England and France fought the Seven Years' War. England gained the land east of the Mississippi River by winning the war. However, the war was very expensive for England. King George III wanted the thirteen American colonies to help **pay off** the government's debt. He made laws the colonists did not like and began to tax goods.

In 1764, the English **Parliament** passed the Sugar Act, and it passed the Stamp Act in 1765. This meant that when the colonists bought sugar, stamps, and paper, they had to pay extra money. The colonists protested. They called them the **Intolerable Acts** and began **boycotting** English goods. They said, "No **taxation** without representation." They wanted **representatives** in Parliament, but the king refused. Soon, fighting began between the English and the colonists.

Many Americans wanted **independence** from England. Tension between the Americans and English soldiers led to the Boston Massacre in 1770. American **minutemen** began training to be ready to fight "at a minute's notice." On April 19, 1775, English soldiers, called redcoats, and American minutemen fought at Lexington and Concord, Massachusetts. These were the first two battles of the **Revolutionary War**. One year later, on July 4, 1776, the Continental Congress signed the Declaration of Independence. They proclaimed that America was an independent country.

George Washington was appointed the commander of the Continental Army. The early years of the war were difficult. After winning the Battle of Saratoga in 1777, the Americans **convinced** France and other European countries to help them. There were many years of fighting. The Americans both won and lost battles. Then, in 1781, the American army and French navy forced General Cornwallis, the English army commander, to **surrender** at Yorktown, Virginia. The war was over. Two years later, England recognized the independence of the American colonies.

▲ minuteman

▲ the Continental Army

▲ the surrender of Burgoyne at Saratoga, 1777

▲ Siege of Yorktown, 1781

▲ the surrender of Cornwallis at Yorktown, Virginia, 1781

Quick Check Check T (True) or F (False).

1 England taxed the American colonists to pay the debt for the Seven Years' War. T F
2 The first battle of the Revolutionary War was at Saratoga. T F
3 George Washington was the commander of the Continental Army. T F

1   What is the passage mainly about?
a. George Washington and the Revolutionary War.
b. The English and French in the Seven Years' War.
c. The period leading up to the Revolutionary War.

2   The British soldiers were often called _____ .
a. redcoats   b. minutemen   c. colonists

3   Who surrendered to the Americans and French at Yorktown?
a. George Washington.   b. General Cornwallis.   c. King George III.

4   What does proclaimed mean?
a. Passed.   b. Declared.   c. Convinced.

5   According to the passage, which statement is true?
a. The Sugar Act was passed by Parliament in 1765.
b. The first battle of the Revolutionary War was fought in 1781.
c. The Battle of Saratoga convinced the French to help the Americans.

6   Complete the outline.

The Prewar Period

- Colonists were taxed heavily to pay for the ᵃ_____ from the Seven Years' War.
- Colonists called the Stamp Act and Sugar Act the Intolerable Acts.
- Colonists said, "No taxation without ᵇ_____."
- No representatives in Parliament

The Revolutionary War

- First battles at Lexington and Concord in 1775
- July 4, 1776 = the ᶜ_____ of Independence was signed
- Americans won the Battle of Saratoga in 1777.
- Americans and French made the English surrender at ᵈ_____ in 1781.
- England recognized America as an ᵉ_____ country in 1783.

Complete each sentence. Change the form if necessary.

pay off	Intolerable Acts	boycott	convince	representative

1   The colonists _____ stamps, tea, sugar, and other taxed products.
2   The Americans desired _____ in the British Parliament but were rejected.
3   The English wanted to _____ their debt from the war.
4   The English could not _____ the Americans to remain colonists.
5   The American colonists hated the _____ _____ and protested them.

A

Complete each sentence with the correct word. Change the form if necessary.

civilization	fairly	based on	scarce	physical environment
interference	densely	dominate	wander	stream into

1   The _____ _____ of a region includes its landforms and climate.

2   The Middle Atlantic has some of the most _____ populated areas in the U.S.

3   The Midwest region is _____ by croplands.

4   Now, all people are treated _____ no matter what race they are.

5   Immigrants _____ _____ the vast empty land in the United States in the 1800s.

6   In a free market, people choose how they earn and spend their money without government _____.

7   When some products are _____, their prices increase.

8   The American economy was once _____ _____ agriculture.

9   The Native Americans had their own _____.

10 In the past, some tribes _____ the land in search of food.

B

Complete each sentence with the correct word. Change the form if necessary.

found	deadly	permanent	colonist	representative
compete	prosper	willing to	claim	Intolerable Acts

1   Europeans _____ to find sea routes to Asia during the Age of Exploration.

2   Europeans were _____ _____ pay high prices for Asia's goods.

3   The cannons and guns of the Spaniards were _____ to the Aztecs.

4   The Spanish _____ much land in the Americas for themselves.

5   Many colonies were _____ by both the English and the French.

6   In 1608, Champlain built a _____ French settlement in present-day Quebec.

7   It took many years before Jamestown began to _____.

8   The _____ boycotted stamps, tea, sugar, and other taxed products.

9   The Americans desired _____ in the British Parliament but were rejected.

10 The American colonists hated the _____ _____ and protested them.

41

Match each word with the correct definition and write the meaning in Chinese.

1   ethnic group _____ ☐

2   immigrant _____ ☐

3   discrimination _____ ☐

4   entrepreneur _____ ☐

5   archaeologist _____ ☐

6   hunter-gatherer _____ ☐

7   expedition _____ ☐

8   circumnavigation_____ ☐

9   conquistador _____ ☐

10 colony _____ ☐

a. a Spanish conqueror
b. a person who starts his or her own business
c. a person who studies past human civilizations
d. the act of traveling completely around the world
e. an area ruled by the government of a faraway country
f. people who share the same customs, language, and history
g. a person who hunts animals and collects vegetation for food
h. a long and carefully organized journey with a specific purpose
i. a person who leaves his or her country to move to another one
j. treating someone poorly because of that person's race, gender, or religion

D

Write the meanings of the words in Chinese.

1	physical environment _____		16	spice _____
2	arid _____		17	caravel _____
3	cash crop _____		18	exploration _____
4	prairie _____		19	Spaniard _____
5	fertile _____		20	capture _____
6	cropland _____		21	permanent _____
7	diverse _____		22	settlement _____
8	multicultural _____		23	claim _____
9	landform _____		24	Puritan _____
10	craft _____		25	immunity _____
11	alliance _____		26	taxation _____
12	opportunity cost _____		27	Revolutionary War _____
13	supply _____		28	independence _____
14	demand _____		29	Parliament _____
15	tribe _____		30	boycott _____

2

● Science

How Are Living Things Classified?

What are the major groups of organisms?

Members of the Animalia Kingdom are multicellular and can move.

Members of the Plantae Kingdom are multicellular but cannot move.

Members of the Fungi Kingdom cannot do photosynthesis at all.

Write the correct word and the meaning in Chinese next to its meaning.

microscopic   multicellular   Protista Kingdom   Plantae Kingdom   feed on

1 _____ : the group of multicellular organisms that cannot move and includes ferns and mosses

2 _____ : the group of organisms that includes amoebas and algae

3 _____ : being so small that one cannot be seen without a microscope

4 _____ : to eat (something)

5 _____ : having more than one cell; multi-celled

The Five Kingdoms of Organisms

🎧 09

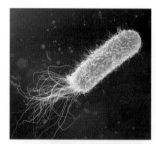

▲ bacteria

▲ amoeba

▲ plantlike algae

Organisms are **classified** by the characteristics they have in common. Ancient scientists grouped all living things as either plants or animals. However, when the microscope was invented, scientists discovered many organisms that needed new **classifications**. Today, scientists classify living things into five large groups called kingdoms. They are the Monera, Protista, Fungi, Plantae, and Animalia kingdoms.

Members of the **Monera Kingdom** are very simple single-celled organisms. They can be seen only with a microscope. They are also called prokaryotes. This means that they **lack** a nucleus in their cells. Bacteria and certain types of algae are in the Monera Kingdom. These organisms get nutrients by absorbing them through their cell walls.

▲ bacterial cell

Organisms in the **Protista**, or Protist, Kingdom are also **microscopic**. Some have animal features, some have plant features, and some have features of both plants and animals.

▲ chloroplast

Most are single-celled, but some have many cells. They include animallike amoebas and plantlike algae. The cells in algae contain chloroplasts. This enables them to do **photosynthesis** and to make their own food.

Organisms in the **Fungi** Kingdom are multi-celled. They include molds, yeasts, and mushrooms. Fungi are similar to plants, but they do not get their nutrition from photosynthesis. Instead, they **feed on** the decaying tissues of other organisms.

Members of the **Plantae**, or Plant, Kingdom are **multicellular** organisms that cannot move. They include ferns, mosses, and flowering and non-flowering plants. Plant cells contain chlorophyll, which makes them green. It also allows them to use photosynthesis to make their own food.

Members of the **Animalia**, or Animal, Kingdom are multicellular organisms that can move. They include insects, worms, fish, reptiles, amphibians, birds, and mammals. Animals cannot create their own food. Instead, they eat other organisms such as plants and animals to get their nutrition.

▲ Monera

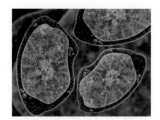

▲ Protista

▲ Fungi

▲ Plantae

▲ Animalia

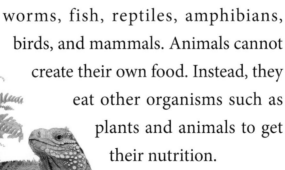

▲ fern

◂ reptile

Quick Check Check T (True) or F (False).

1	Members of the Monera Kingdom have more than one cell.	☐ T ☐ F
2	Non-flowering plants belong to the Fungi Kingdom.	☐ T ☐ F
3	Members of the Animalia Kingdom include birds and reptiles.	☐ T ☐ F

1 **What is the main idea of the passage?**
   a. The Animal and Plant kingdoms are more complex than the other kingdoms.
   b. All organisms can be classified into five different kingdoms.
   c. There is an amazing variety of life on Earth.

2 **Amoebas belong to the _____ Kingdom.**
   a. Protista   **b.** Monera   **c.** Fungi

3 **What is one characteristic of members of the Plantae Kingdom?**
   a. They can do photosynthesis.
   b. They are able to move.
   c. They are all microscopic.

4 **What does decaying mean?**
   a. Transmitting.   **b.** Rotting.   **c.** Living.

5 **Complete the sentences.**
   a. Prokaryotes _____ nutrients through their cell walls.
   b. Protists like _____ contain chloroplasts, so they can do photosynthesis.
   c. Animals are unable to make their own _____.

6 **Complete the outline.**

Simple Organisms
Prokaryotes • Are single-celled organisms • Can be seen through a ᵃ_____ • Include ᵇ_____ and some algae Protists • Are microscopic • Include ᶜ_____ and algae

Complex Organisms
Fungi • Include molds, yeasts, and ᵈ_____ • Feed on decaying tissue Plants • ᵉ_____ organisms that cannot move Animals • Multicellular organisms that can move

Complete each sentence. Change the form if necessary.

classified by	classification	photosynthesis	feed on	lack

1 All members of the Plantae Kingdom can do _____.

2 Many animals _____ _____ other animals for nourishment.

3 All organisms are _____ _____ their various characteristics.

4 Organisms in the Plantae Kingdom _____ the ability to move.

5 One _____ of organisms is the Animalia Kingdom.

Classification

What are the different levels of classification?

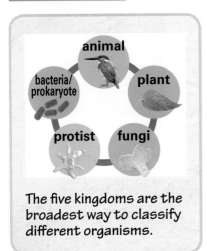

The five kingdoms are the broadest way to classify different organisms.

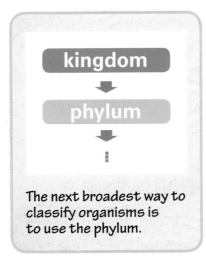

The next broadest way to classify organisms is to use the phylum.

Every species of humans belongs to the genus *Homo,* which means "man."

Write the correct word and the meaning in Chinese next to its meaning.

phylum	genus	related	precise	specify

1 _____ : to explain something in an exact and detailed way

2 _____ : the category of classification directly after kingdom

3 _____ : connected in some way; connected by a family relationship

4 _____ : a closely related group of organisms

5 _____ : exact and accurate

The Seven Levels of Classification

▲ Carl Linnaeus

There may be millions of organisms on the planet that we do not know anything about. If you discovered a new living thing, what would you name it? How would you classify it? Long ago, scientists around the world had trouble communicating about the organisms they were studying. They spoke different languages, so they called the same organisms different names. Swedish scientist Carl Linnaeus **took care of** this problem. He grouped all organisms into seven levels and gave them Latin names, so all scientists would understand the names. Today, we still use the **Linnaean System** as the **basis** for classifying living things.

Scientists now classify all living things into seven levels. They are kingdom, phylum, class, order, family, genus, and species. At each level, all organisms share particular characteristics.

The highest level is kingdom. Each kingdom can contain several phyla, each phylum can contain several classes, and so on. The classification gets more specific as it goes down.

All organisms belong to one of five kingdoms: Monera, Protista, Fungi, Plantae, and Animalia. The next category is the **phylum**. Organisms that belong to the same phylum have similar body plans. For instance, the Animalia Kingdom has 33 phyla. One is *Chordata*. Chordates are animals with backbones.

50

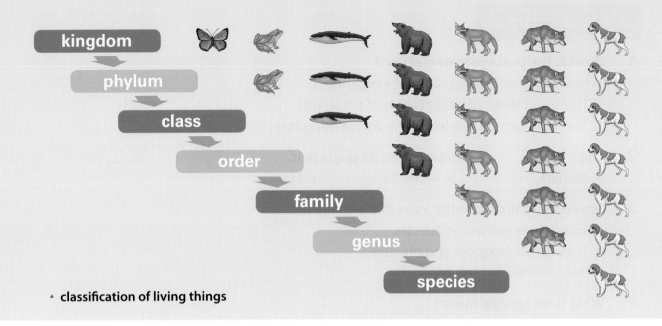

▲ **classification of living things**

Classes, orders, and families further divide organisms. In the *Chordata* phylum, there are several classes. They include mammals, reptiles, birds, amphibians, and fish. In the *Mammalia* class, animals may belong to certain orders **depending on** the food they eat. So there are orders for carnivores, herbivores, and other types of animals. In the order *Carnivora*, there are families for animals such as dogs, cats, and bears.

The last two categories are genus and species. A **genus** is a group of organisms that is closely **related**. **Species** is the most **precise** classification. Members of a species share at least one characteristic that no other organisms have.

The way an organism is classified **determines** its scientific name. When scientists want to **specify** an organism, they typically use the genus and the species. The first part of the name tells its genus. The second part of the name tells its species. For example, the scientific name for human beings is *Homo sapiens*. *Homo* is the genus, and *sapiens* is the species.

Altogether, the way an organism is classified provides a lot of information about it. It allows people to note the similarities and differences between various organisms.

Quick Check Check T (True) or F (False).

1   There are 33 phyla in the Animal Kingdom.   T   F
2   The order *Carnivora* contains dogs, cats, and bears.   T   F
3   The genus for modern humans is *sapiens*.   T   F

1 **What is the passage mainly about?**
a. How Carl Linnaeus classified the organisms.
b. The seven levels of classification of organisms.
c. The most common orders in the Animal Kingdom.

2 **The _____ Kingdom has 33 phyla in it.**
a. Monera   b. Animalia   c. Plantae

3 **How do scientists identify a specific organism?**
a. They use its genus and species.
b. They use its kingdom and phylum.
c. They use its class and order.

4 **What does specific mean?**
a. Closed.   b. Basic.   c. Precise.

5 **According to the passage, which statement is true?**
a. There are six kingdoms of organisms.
b. Mammals, reptiles, and birds are all classes of animals.
c. The genus and species for modern humans is Homo erectus.

6 **Complete the outline.**

Broad Classifications
• Kingdom = the highest level of ^a _____
• Phylum = contains organisms with similar body plans
• Class = divides organisms even further
• ^b _____ = may divide animals according to what they eat
• ^c _____ = smaller groups of organisms

Specific Classifications
• Genus = A group of organisms that are closely ^d _____.
• Species = The organism in it has one or more ^e _____ that no other organism has.

Complete each sentence. Change the form if necessary.

take care of   basis   depend on   determine   specify

1   The scientist must _____ what kind of animal that is.

2   Grouping organisms _____ _____ the traits they have.

3   Please _____ the genus and species of this animal.

4   The scientists will _____ _____ _____ the experiments in their laboratory.

5   What is the _____ for calling this organism a plant?

Unit 11 How Plants Meet Their Needs

Visual Preview What are the three major parts of a plant?

Plants' roots help anchor them to the ground and absorb water and nutrients.

The stem supports the plant and takes water and nutrients to the leaves.

The leaves collect sunlight and perform photosynthesis to make the plant's food.

Vocabulary Preview Write the correct word and the meaning in Chinese next to its meaning.

| respiration | anchor | xylem | chloroplast | photosynthesis |

1 _____ : the part of a plant that moves water and minerals up to the stem

2 _____ : a part of a plant cell that contains chlorophyll and where photosynthesis takes place

3 _____ : to fix something firmly somewhere

4 _____ : the process that plants use to create food for themselves

5 _____ : the process of breathing air in and out

Plant Structures and Functions

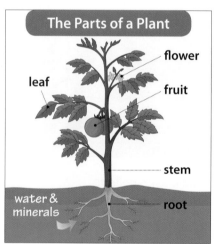

The Parts of a Plant

flower

leaf

fruit

stem

water & minerals

root

The Parts of a Root

root hairs

epidermis

cortex

xylem

cambium

phloem

All plants have basic needs. They need sunlight, water, air, and nutrients to live and grow. To meet their needs, all plants have certain parts with the same **functions**.

Plants have roots that hold them in the ground. Roots help **anchor** a plant in the soil and **prevent** the plant from moving. Roots are **responsible for** absorbing water and minerals from the soil. The structure of a root helps it absorb water and minerals and send them to the other parts of the plant.

In most plants, tiny root hairs take in water and minerals from the soil. The water and minerals pass through the root's cortex and enter the **xylem**. Then, they move upward through the xylem to the plant's stem and to all the parts of the plant.

54

Stems support leaves and flowers. Some stems, like those on trees, are huge and hard. Other stems, like those on flowers, are much smaller and soft. Yet all stems have the same basic parts for holding the **transportation system** of plants. The xylem in the stem moves water and minerals up from the roots. The **phloem** moves food from the plant's leaves to all the parts of the plant.

Some stems do more than transporting. Some stems, like in potatoes, store food for the plants to use later. In fact, the potatoes we eat are underground stems. In addition, the stems of cacti store water during long dry periods in the desert.

Leaves are the green parts of a plant. Leaves are green because they contain chlorophyll. Chlorophyll is found in chloroplasts. It lets plants undergo **photosynthesis**. This is the food-making process of plants. Plants need water, carbon dioxide, and sunlight to undergo photosynthesis. Inside the **chloroplasts**, water and carbon dioxide combine to make sugar and oxygen. The plants then use this sugar to live and grow. During photosynthesis, plants release oxygen into the air, so other organisms can breathe it. Then, during **respiration**, which occurs in plants and animals, the water and carbon dioxide are released into the air.

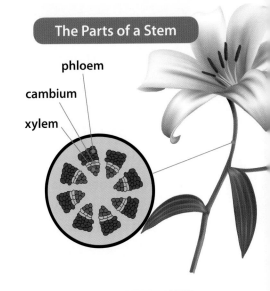

The Parts of a Stem

phloem
cambium
xylem

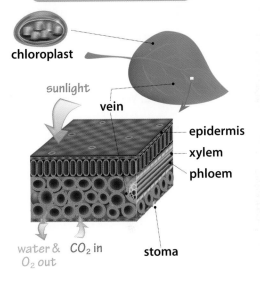

The Parts of a Leaf

chloroplast
sunlight
vein
epidermis
xylem
phloem
water & O_2 out CO_2 in
stoma

▲ **cactus (*pl.* cacti/cactuses)**

Quick Check   Check T (True) or F (False).

1   The roots of a plant absorb water from the ground.   ☐T ☐F

2   The stem can create food by using chloroplasts.   ☐T ☐F

3   The leaves are the part of the plant that undergoes photosynthesis.   ☐T ☐F

1   What is the main idea of the passage?
   a. Roots, stems, and leaves all have important functions.
   b. Without chloroplasts, plants could not undergo photosynthesis.
   c. Plants need sunlight, water, air, and nutrients to live.

2   The part of the plant that supports the leaves and flowers is the _____.
   a. roots   **b.** stem   **c.** leaves

3   What does a plant do during photosynthesis?
   a. It releases oxygen into the air.
   b. It creates water for other plants to use.
   c. It releases carbon dioxide into the air.

4   What does absorbing mean?
   a. Soaking to.   **b.** Soaking up.   **c.** Soaking with.

5   Answer the questions.
   a. Which part of a plant moves food from the leaves to the rest of it?

   _____

   b. What do the stems of potatoes do? _____

   c. What is photosynthesis? _____

6   Complete the outline.

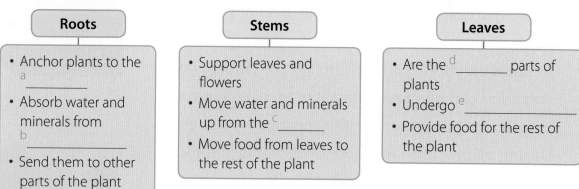

Roots	Stems	Leaves
• Anchor plants to the ^{a}_____	• Support leaves and flowers	• Are the ^{d}_____ parts of plants
• Absorb water and minerals from ^{b}_____	• Move water and minerals up from the ^{c}_____	• Undergo ^{e}_____
• Send them to other parts of the plant	• Move food from leaves to the rest of the plant	• Provide food for the rest of the plant

Complete each sentence. Change the form if necessary.

| function   anchor   prevent   responsible for   chloroplast |

1   The roots of a plant _____ it to the ground.

2   _____ are necessary for a plant to undergo photosynthesis.

3   The phloem is _____ _____ moving food to all of the parts of the plant.

4   The stem of a plant has several different _____.

5   Plants' roots _____ them from being blown away by the wind.

How Do Plants Reproduce?

Visual Preview — What are some parts of a plant's reproductive system?

The anther is the male part that has the pollen.

The pistil is the female part that includes the stigma.

When pollen reaches the stigma, the egg cells can be fertilized.

Vocabulary Preview — Write the correct word and the meaning in Chinese next to its meaning.

| pollen | reproductive | germinate | fertilization | pollination |

1. _____ : tiny grains that are responsible for fertilizing a flower's egg cells

2. _____ : to develop from a seed and begin to grow into a plant, or to make a seed develop in this way

3. _____ : relating to or involved in the production of babies, young animals, or new plants

4. _____ : the transfer of pollen from the anther to the stigma

5. _____ : the process of fertilizing; the states of being fertilized

Flowers and Seeds

🎧 12

▲ a bee covered with pollen

Most plants make seeds from their flowers. Flowers are the **reproductive** organs in the plants. Thanks to them, plants can produce seeds that will develop and grow into new plants.

Flowers have male parts and female parts. The male parts make **pollen**. The female parts make egg cells that become seeds.

The **stamen** is a flower's male part. A stamen has two parts. The anther produces pollen grains. The filament is the stalk that connects the anther to the plant. The **pistil** is the flower's female part. The pistil has three parts. At its top is the stigma. The stigma captures the pollen grains that fall on it. The stem-like part in the middle is the style. The ovary is the base of the flower

The Parts of a Flower

stigma

pistil style

ovary

petal

anther
filament stamen

sepal

that contains egg cells. The egg cells develop into seeds if they are **fertilized**.

To make seeds, a plant must be **pollinated** first. **Pollination** occurs when a pollen grain is **transferred** from the anther to the stigma. This can happen through self-pollination or cross-pollination. If the pollen is transferred in the same flower, it is called self-pollination. If the pollen is transferred from the anther of one flower to the stigma of another flower, it is called cross-pollination. This is where the flower petals are useful. Flower petals are the colorful outer coverings of flowers. They attract bees, butterflies, hummingbirds, or other animals. As they go from flower to flower, some pollen gets stuck on them. The pollen then gets transferred to other flowers. That is how many flowers get pollinated.

▲ **Bees and butterflies help pollination.**

Once a flower gets pollinated, a pollen tube starts to grow, and it goes down into the ovary until it reaches an egg cell. Then, **fertilization** occurs, and a seed forms. The seed contains an embryo of a new plant. The seed first develops into a fruit, which may have one or more seeds. Many of these seeds later fall to the ground. When that happens, they may **germinate** and grow into new plants.

The Pollination of a Flower

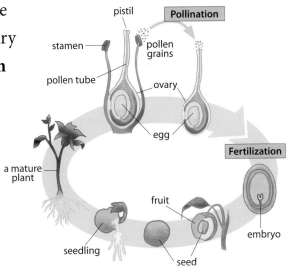

Quick Check   Check T (True) or F (False).

1   The anther is a part of the pistil.   T   F
2   Flowers can be self-pollinated or cross-pollinated.   T   F
3   Many times, animals such as bees and butterflies pollinate flowers.   T   F

1 **What is the passage mainly about?**
a. What kinds of plants produce flowers.
b. How plants get fertilized.
c. When flowers are able to be pollinated.

2 **The top of the pistil is called the _____.**
a. anther   b. ovary   c. stigma

3 **What happens when a flower gets pollinated?**
a. An animal cross-pollinates the flower.
b. A pollen tube begins to grow.
c. The seeds fall to the ground.

4 **What does base mean?**
a. Bottom.   b. Middle.   c. Top.

5 **Complete the sentences.**
a. The _____ organs of a plant are its flowers.
b. In _____, pollen is transferred in the same flower.
c. A seed has an _____ of a new plant.

6 **Complete the outline.**

The Parts of a Flower
a _____ = the male part
• Anther = produces pollen
• Filament = the stalk
b _____ = the female part
• Stigma = the top of the pistil
• Style = the stem-like part in the middle
• c _____ = the base of the flower that contains egg cells

Pollination of a Flower
• Pollen grain gets transferred from the anther to the d _____.
• Can be through self- or e _____
• A f _____ _____ grows down to the ovary.
• An egg cell gets fertilized.
• A seed begins to grow.
• The seed develops into a fruit that has its own seeds.

Complete each sentence. Change the form if necessary.

reproductive   fertilize   pollinate   transfer   germinate

1 Bees and hummingbirds are often responsible for _____ flowers.

2 When a seed _____, it can grow into a plant.

3 The stigma is part of a plant's _____ system.

4 The wind can help _____ pollen from the anther to the stigma.

5 Unless an egg cell gets _____, it cannot become a seed.

13 What Are Some Types of Plants?

What are some kinds of plants that produce seeds?

Angiosperms are plants that produce both flowers and seeds.

The majority of plants on the earth are angiosperms.

Pine trees are gymnosperms, so they produce seeds but not flowers or fruits.

Vocabulary Preview Write the correct word and the meaning in Chinese next to its meaning.

| angiosperm | gymnosperm | monocot | seed leaf | reproduce |

1 _____ : a flowering plant with an embryo that bears a single cotyledon

2 _____ : a plant that produces flowers and fruits

3 _____ : a cotyledon

4 _____ : a plant that produces seeds but not flowers or fruits

5 _____ : to produce babies, young animals, new plants, etc.

Plants With Seeds

🎧 13

seed   fruit

The majority of plants have seeds. There are two major groups of **seed plants**: angiosperms and gymnosperms.

Most plants on the earth are **angiosperms**. Flowers, grasses, crops, and most trees are all angiosperms. Angiosperms, also known as flowering plants, produce flowers and fruits. Their seeds are surrounded by fruits. The fruit protects the seeds inside it. Fruits of all angiosperms form from flowers, the plants' reproductive organs.

Scientists divide angiosperms into two groups that are based on how many **seed leaves** a plant's seed has. Monocotyledons, or **monocots**, have one seed leaf, also called a cotyledon. Dicotyledons, or dicots, have two seed leaves.

Angiosperms live in all climates and in all parts of the world. They are the largest division in the Plant Kingdom.

seed leaf

monocot   dicot

Gymnosperms produce seeds but have no flowers or fruits. The seeds are not surrounded by a fruit. They produce seeds on cones. Most gymnosperms are evergreens and have narrow, needlelike leaves. One kind of gymnosperm is the **conifer**, which includes pine, cedar, and cypress trees. Cycads and gingkoes are two other kinds of gymnosperms.

Instead of having flowers and fruits, gymnosperms **reproduce** in other ways. For example, conifers, such as pine trees, often have both male and female cones on a tree. Male cones release pollen grains, which contain **sperm cells**. The female cones produce egg cells. When the pollen grains get carried by the wind and happen to land on a female cone, the sperm cells from the pollen join with **egg cells**. The fertilized eggs eventually become a seed. When the seeds mature, the female cones fall from the tree and scatter them on the ground. The wind or water often carries the seeds away from the tree. When the conditions are right, the seeds germinate and grow into new pine trees.

Gymnosperms are the oldest seed plants. Millions of years ago, they were the **dominant** plants on the earth. Today, there are only around 700 species of gymnosperms.

▲ **angiosperm**

▲ **gymnosperm**

▲ **Male cones release pollen grains.**

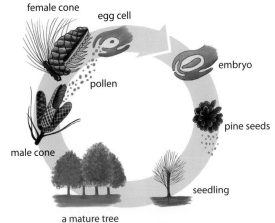
female cone
egg cell
embryo
pollen
pine seeds
male cone
seedling
a mature tree

The Life Cycle of a Gymnosperm

Quick Check Check T (True) or F (False).

1 All angiosperms can be divided into monocots or dicots. T F

2 Gymnosperms are plants that produce flowers, fruits, and seeds. T F

3 Conifers, gingkoes, and cycads are all examples of gymnosperms. T F

1 **What is the passage mainly about?**
   a. Why there are more angiosperms than gymnosperms.
   b. The manner in which gymnosperms reproduce.
   c. The different kinds of plants that produce seeds.

2 **There are around _____ species of gymnosperms on the planet today.**
   a. 100   **b.** 700   **c.** 1,000,000

3 **How does pollen from a male cone transfer to a female cone in a gymnosperm?**
   a. By the wind.   **b.** By insects.   **c.** By birds.

4 **What does scatter mean?**
   a. Move.   **b.** Carry.   **c.** Spread.

5 **According to the passage, which statement is true?**
   a. Flowers, crops, and grasses are all gymnosperms.
   b. Pine trees, cycads, and gingkoes are all angiosperms.
   c. Gymnosperms used to dominate the earth but are now less common.

6 **Complete the outline.**

Angiosperms
- Are flowers, grasses, crops, and most trees
- Produce ᵃ_____ and fruits
- Have seeds surrounded by ᵇ_____
- Are either monocots or ᶜ_____
- Live everywhere in the world
- Are the largest division in the Plant Kingdom

Gymnosperms
- Are seed plants but have no flowers or fruits
- Produce seeds on ᵈ_____
- Are ᵉ_____ like pine, cedar, and cypress trees
- Cycads and gingkoes are two other kinds of gymnosperms.
- Have both male and female cones
- Get pollinated through the wind

Complete each sentence. Change the form if necessary.

monocot	reproduce	sperm cell	egg cell	dominant

1 Angiosperms _____ by having flowers and fruits that produce seeds.

2 _____ have one seed leaf.

3 _____ _____ are contained in pollen, which fertilizes female cones.

4 Gymnosperms are no longer the most _____ plants on the planet.

5 When an _____ _____ is touched by pollen, it can be fertilized.

Plants Without Seeds

Visual Preview What are some features of seedless plants?

They are either vascular plants or nonvascular plants.

They use spores to reproduce.

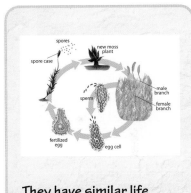

They have similar life cycles.

Vocabulary Preview Write the correct word and the meaning in Chinese next to its meaning.

spore   lack   vascular plant   seedless   asexual reproduction

1 _____ : a plant that has tissues that carry food and nutrients

2 _____ : not containing any seeds

3 _____ : to be deficient or missing

4 _____ : the part of a fern or a moss that lets it reproduce

5 _____ : reproduction without male or female parts

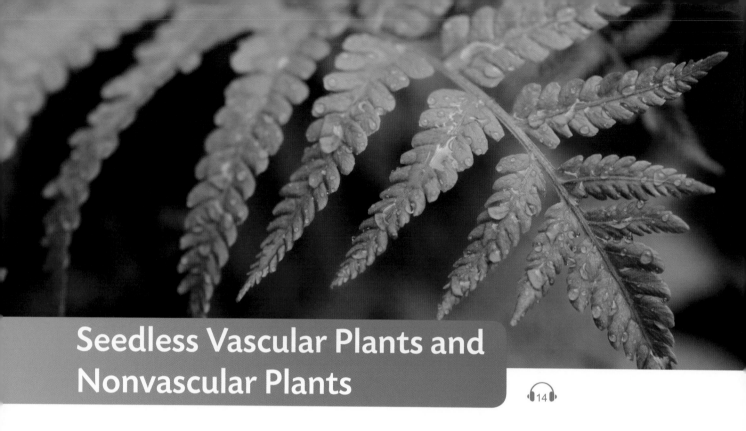

Seedless Vascular Plants and Nonvascular Plants

🎧 14

▲ seedless nonvascular plant

▲ seedless vascular plant

Most plants reproduce with seeds, but not all of them do. Some reproduce without using seeds. We can divide these **seedless** plants into two groups: seedless **vascular plants** and seedless **nonvascular plants**.

Vascular plants have vascular tissues that are made of tubelike cells. These tissues let water and nutrients move through the roots and stems. All angiosperms and gymnosperms are vascular plants. Nonvascular plants, however, **lack** these tissues.

Mosses are the most **common** types of seedless nonvascular plants. These plants all use photosynthesis to provide nutrition for themselves. However, they lack the veins that vascular plants have. This lack of veins prevents nonvascular plants from growing very large and also makes them grow close to the ground.

◂ frond

Ferns are the most common type of seedless vascular plants. These are very old plants that once thrived millions of years ago. Ferns have leaves that are called **fronds**. They grow from the underground stem called a rhizome. Ferns have vascular tissues, so they can grow tall and thick.

▲ **spore**

Both mosses and ferns reproduce without seeds. They use **spores** to make new plants, so their life cycles are alike. Both mosses and ferns have two separate stages in their life cycles.

Let's look at the life cycle of mosses. In the first stage, mosses produce spores **asexually**. When the spore case opens, the spores are released. Spores that land on damp ground grow into new plants. This stage is called **asexual reproduction**. As mosses develop, they have male branches and female branches. The male branches produce sperm, and the female branches produce eggs. When there is enough moisture, the sperm cells move to the eggs and fertilize them. Each fertilized egg produces a stalk that develops a capsule, called a spore case, which is filled with spores. This second stage is called **sexual reproduction.** The life cycle of ferns is very similar to that of mosses.

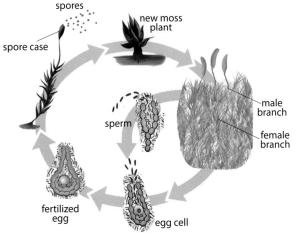

The Life Cycle of a Moss

▲ **spore capsule/case**

Quick Check Check T (True) or F (False).

1 The most common seedless nonvascular plants are ferns.   T   F

2 Ferns have been on the earth for millions of years.   T   F

3 Mosses and ferns reproduce without the use of seeds.   T   F

1 **What is the passage mainly about?**
a. Seedless plants.
b. Vascular Plants.
c. Nonvascular Plants.

2 **Ferns reproduce in the first stage through _____.**
a. sexual reproduction　　b. self-fertilization　　c. asexual reproduction

3 **What is a rhizome?**
a. A kind of seedless vascular plant.
b. The underground stem of a fern.
c. The grassy part of a moss.

4 **What does prevents mean?**
a. Stops.　　　　b. Makes.　　　　c. Permits.

5 **Answer the questions.**
a. What kinds of plants are vascular plants? _____
b. Why can ferns grow to be tall? _____
c. What do mosses use to reproduce? _____

6 **Complete the outline.**

Vascular Plants With Seeds
• Are plants with vascular ᵃ_____   • Include all angiosperms and ᵇ_____

Seedless Plants
Seedless Nonvascular Plants   • Lack vascular tissues   • Include mosses   • Reproduce by using ᶜ_____   • Have two stages in their life cycles: asexual reproduction and ᵈ_____ reproduction   **Seedless Vascular Plants**   • Include ferns   • Have very similar ᵉ_____ _____ to mosses

Complete each sentence. Change the form if necessary.

seedless　　lack　　common　　asexually　　sexual reproduction

1 Nonvascular plants _____ vascular tissues to transport food and nutrients.

2 _____ _____ involves both male and female parts.

3 Ferns are not as _____ as they used to be on the planet.

4 _____ plants do not reproduce by producing fruits.

5 Mosses reproduce _____ in their first stage of reproduction.

Plant Responses and Adaptations

What are some ways that plants adapt to their environments?

A plant grows or bends toward sunlight.

The roots of plants grow toward water so that they can get nourishment.

Many cacti can store water to survive during dry periods.

Vocabulary Preview **Write the correct word and the meaning in Chinese next to its meaning.**

| stimulus | tropism | carnivorous | involuntary | phototropism |

1 _____ : a response of a plant toward a various condition

2 _____ : an external force that affects an organism in some way

3 _____ : the growing of a plant toward sunlight

4 _____ : subsisting on nutrients obtained from the breakdown of animal protoplasm (as of insects)

5 _____ : not done or made consciously

How Do Plants Respond to Their Environments?

🎧15

▲ phototropism

negative

positive

▲ gravitropism

All living things have adaptations that help them survive. Plants also respond to their environments to survive, but they **tend to** respond more slowly than animals do. **Tropisms** and other responses to certain conditions help plants meet their needs.

A plant's response to an external **stimulus** is called a tropism. There are several types of tropisms. One is **phototropism**. In phototropism, plants grow or bend toward sunlight. This enables plants to get as much light as possible so that they may undergo photosynthesis. Another is **gravitropism**. This is how plants respond to gravity. Plants' roots respond to the stimulus of gravity, so they grow downward into the soil while their stems and leaves grow up in the air. **Hydrotropism** is the response of plants to water. Plants—especially their roots—grow toward a source of water.

▲ hydrotropism

▲ cacti

Venus flytrap

tropical pitcher plant

sundew

▲ carnivorous plants

Tropisms are all **involuntary** responses by plants. They may be either positive or negative. For instance, the roots of a plant that grow down in the direction of gravity show positive gravitropism. Stems that grow away from the pull of gravity show negative gravitropism.

Plants have also adapted to their environments in many ways. For instance, desert environments are very dry and get little water. So **cacti** and other desert plants have adapted to the weather. They can endure long periods of time without water and can also store large amounts of water inside them when it rains. Also, some plants that get little sunlight have adapted by becoming **carnivorous**. Plants like the Venus flytrap **sustain** themselves by capturing and eating small insects. In this way, they can get enough nutrition to survive.

Quick Check   Check T (True) or F (False).

1   The roots of plants tend to grow in the direction of water.   T   F

2   All tropisms are positive factors for plants.   T   F

3   The roots of the Venus flytrap can store large amounts of water.   T   F

1   What is the main idea of the passage?
a. There are several different types of tropisms.
b. A few plants become carnivorous to get nutrition.
c. Plants respond to an external stimulus and their environments.

2   One example of _____ is a plant bending in the direction of light.
a. hydrotropism   b. phototropism   c. gravitropism

3   How have cacti adapted to their environments?
a. They can go for long periods of time without water.
b. Their roots grow down toward the ground.
c. They sometimes eat small animals.

4   What does endure mean?
a. Bear.   b. Express.   c. Live.

5   Complete the sentences.
a. Plants respond to their environments more _____ than animals.
b. _____ can be both positive and negative.
c. A plant that gets little sunlight might become _____ and eat small animals.

6   Complete the outline.

Tropisms
• Are the ^{a}_____ of plants to various stimuli
• Phototropism = the growing or bending of a plant toward ^{b}_____
• Gravitropism = the growing downward of roots and upward of stems and leaves
• ^{c}_____ = the growing of a plant's roots toward water

Adaptations
• Desert plants can go for long periods of time with no ^{d}_____.
• Cacti can store water for later use.
• Venus ^{e}_____ = a carnivorous plant that gets nutrition by eating small insects

Complete each sentence. Change the form if necessary.

cactus   tend to   involuntary   carnivorous   sustain

1   Plants' roots _____ _____ grow toward a source of water.

2   A _____ plant eats small insects to gain nutrition.

3   Any kind of _____ response to a stimulus by a plant is called a tropism.

4   Some plants can _____ themselves with little water or sunlight.

5   A _____ is a desert plant that does not need much water to survive.

A

Complete each sentence with the correct word. Change the form if necessary.

Fungi	Monera	chloroplast	classified by	prevent
specify	related	respiration	responsible for	basis

1 Organisms are _____ _____ the characteristics they have in common.

2 Members of the _____ Kingdom are very simple single-celled organisms.

3 Organisms in the _____ Kingdom feed on the decaying tissues of other organisms.

4 We still use the Linnaean System as the _____ for classifying living things.

5 A genus is a group of organisms that is closely _____.

6 When scientists want to _____ an organism, they typically use the genus and the species.

7 Plants' roots _____ them from being blown away by the wind.

8 The phloem is _____ _____ moving food to all of the parts of the plant.

9 Inside the _____, water and carbon dioxide combine to make sugar and oxygen.

10 During _____, the water and carbon dioxide are released into the air.

B

Complete each sentence with the correct word. Change the form if necessary.

pollinate	sustain	monocot	egg cell	sexual reproduction
asexually	lack	dominant	transfer	reproductive

1 Bees and hummingbirds are often responsible for _____ flowers.

2 The wind can help _____ pollen from the anther to the stigma.

3 When an _____ _____ is touched by pollen, it can be fertilized.

4 Gymnosperms are no longer the most _____ plants on the planet.

5 Nonvascular plants _____ vascular tissues to transport food and nutrients.

6 _____ _____ involves both male and female parts.

7 Mosses reproduce _____ in their first stage of reproduction.

8 The stigma is part of a plant's _____ system.

9 _____ have one seed leaf.

10 Some plants can _____ themselves with little water or sunlight.

Match each word with the correct definition and write the meaning in Chinese.

1   Protist Kingdom _____ ☐

2   microscopic _____ ☐

3   phylum _____ ☐

4   genus _____ ☐

5   species _____ ☐

6   angiosperm _____ ☐

7   xylem _____ ☐

8   gymnosperm _____ ☐

9   vascular plant _____ ☐

10 phototropism _____ ☐

a. a plant that produces flowers and fruits
b. a closely related group of organisms
c. the growing of a plant toward sunlight
d. the most precise classification for an organism
e. the category of classification directly after kingdom
f. a plant that produces seeds but not flowers or fruits
g. the part of a plant that moves water and minerals up to the stem
h. a plant that has tissues that carry food and nutrients
i. the group of organisms that includes amoebas and algae
j. being so small that one cannot be seen without a microscope

D

Write the meanings of the words in Chinese.

1   Monera Kingdom _____

2   Fungi Kingdom _____

3   multicellular _____

4   classification _____

5   involuntary _____

6   depend on _____

7   specify _____

8   take care of _____

9   anchor _____

10 dominant _____

11 chloroplast _____

12 photosynthesis _____

13 function _____

14 transportation system _____

15 phloem _____

16 respiration _____

17 pollen _____

18 stamen _____

19 pistil _____

20 pollination _____

21 fertilization _____

22 seed plant _____

23 seed leaf _____

24 cotyledon _____

25 conifer _____

26 nonvascular plant _____

27 spore _____

28 asexual reproduction _____

29 tropism _____

30 stimulus _____

3

- **Mathematics**
- **Language**
- **Visual Arts**
- **Music**

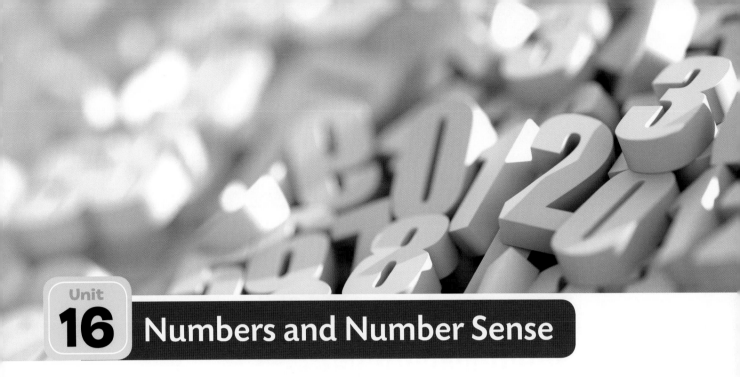

Unit 16 Numbers and Number Sense

How do we use numbers nowadays?

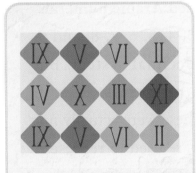

The Romans used to use letters such as I, V, X, and C to stand for numbers.

Today, we use the Arabic numerals 0, 1, 2, 3, 4, 5, 6, 7, 8, and 9.

Numbers can be positive, negative, or zero.

Vocabulary Preview   Write the correct word and the meaning in Chinese next to its meaning.

| Roman numeral | whole number | Arabic numeral | positive integer | odd number |

1 _____ : a number such as 0, 1, 2, 3, 4, 5, 6, 7, 8, or 9

2 _____ : a letter such as I, V, X, or C that stands for a number

3 _____ : a number that is neither a fraction nor a decimal

4 _____ : a number that end in 1, 3, 5, 7, or 9

5 _____ : a number such as 1, 2, 3, 4, or 5

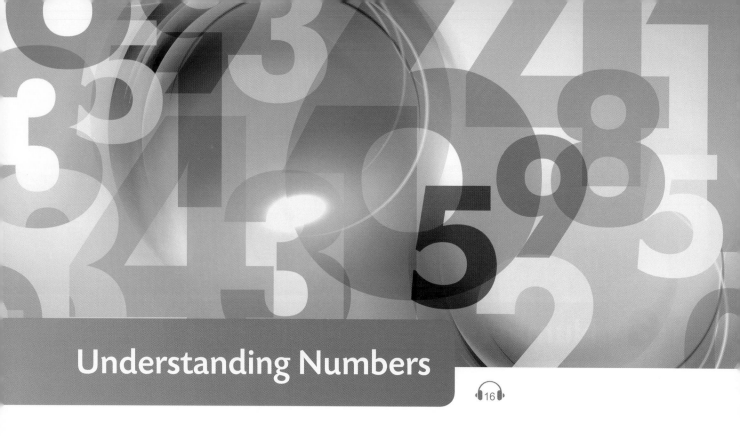

🎧 16

The numerals we use today are called **Arabic numerals**. They are the ten digits 0, 1, 2, 3, 4, 5, 6, 7, 8, and 9. Arabic numerals are based on the **decimal system**. But sometimes we encounter **Roman numerals**. Roman numerals were used by the Romans. These were actually not numbers but letters or symbols that were used to **represent** numbers. Each letter represented a different numerical value. The letters and numbers that they represented were this:

I = 1	V = 5	X = 10	L = 50
C = 100	D = 500	M = 1,000	

To make larger numbers, there were two rules. If the same size or a smaller letter comes after another letter, you add their values together. A letter cannot **repeat** more than 3 times. So II is 1+1, or 2. III is 1+1+1, or 3. VI is 5+1, or 6. If the smaller letter comes right before the larger letter, you subtract the smaller one from the larger one. So, IV is 5–1, or 4. IX is 10–1, or 9. XL is 50–10, or 40. This was extremely **complicated** and made doing math problems very difficult. Imagine trying to multiply CCXII and XXXVI together.

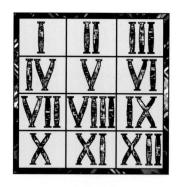

▾ **Roman numerals**

I = 1		II = 2	
III = 3		IV = 4	
V = 5		VI = 6	
VII = 7		VIII = 8	
IX = 9		X = 10	
L = 50		C = 100	
D = 500		M = 1,000	

Fortunately, we use Arabic numerals today. Solving math problems with Arabic numerals is much easier than with Roman numerals.

Let's learn more about numbers. Numbers can be positive or negative. We can show them on a number line. Numbers to the right of 0 are positive. Numbers to the left of 0 are negative. The number 0 is neither positive nor negative.

▲ fraction

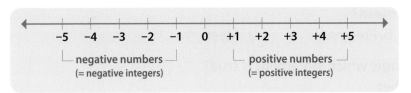

We call these numbers **whole numbers** or **integers**. Numbers with decimals, like 0.2, 3.14, and 10.5 are not whole numbers. Neither are fractions or mixed numbers such as $\frac{1}{2}$ and $4\frac{3}{4}$.

▲ decimal

Integers that are farther to the right on the number line are greater ($+5 > +3$). Integers that are farther to the left on the number line are less ($-1 > -100$). A **positive integer** is always greater than a **negative integer** ($1 > -100$).

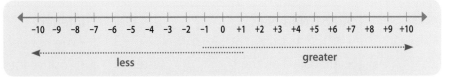

▲ comparing integers

Another way to divide numbers is to **categorize** them as **even** and **odd numbers**. Even numbers are any numbers that end in 0, 2, 4, 6, or 8. 14 is an even number. So are 36 and 42. Odd numbers are any numbers that end in 1, 3, 5, 7, or 9. 11, 53, and 117 are all odd numbers.

odd numbers

even numbers

Quick Check Check T (True) or F (False).

1   Using Roman numerals was very complicated.　　　　　　　T　　F

2   A positive integer is a whole number greater than zero.　　T　　F

3   A decimal can be a whole number.　　　　　　　　　　　T　　F

1 **What is the passage mainly about?**
  a. Whole numbers.
  b. Numerals and integers.
  c. Dividing numbers into even and odd numbers.

2 **A whole number less than zero is a _____.**
  a. decimal   **b.** fraction   **c.** negative integer

3 **How do you write the number 40 in Roman numerals?**
  a. XXXX.   **b.** XL.   **c.** LC.

4 **What does encounter mean?**
  a. Represent.   **b.** Present.   **c.** Meet.

5 **According to the passage, which statement is true?**
  a. 3.14 is a whole number.
  b. Odd numbers end in 0, 2, 4, 6, or 8.
  c. Integers include positive integers, negative integers, and zero.

6 **Complete the outline.**

Numerals

Arabic Numerals
- 0, 1, 2, 3, 4, 5, 6, 7, 8, and 9
- Are based on the ^{a}_____ system

Roman Numerals
- I, V, X, L, C, D, and M
- Were used by the ^{b}_____
- Were very complicated

Integers

Integers
- Are not decimals or ^{c}_____
- Positive integer > 0
- Negative integer < 0
- Zero = 0

^{d}_____ Numbers
- Any numbers that end in 0, 2, 4, 6, or 8

Odd Numbers
- Any numbers that ^{e}____ ____ 1, 3, 5, 7, or 9

Complete each sentence. Change the form if necessary.

represent   odd number   repeat   decimal system   categorize

1 The same Roman numeral could _____ up to three times in a row.

2 All integers can be _____ as positive or negative.

3 In Roman numerals, the letter M _____ 1,000.

4 The _____ _____ is based on the number ten.

5 Numbers such as 1, 3, 5, 7, or 9 are _____ _____.

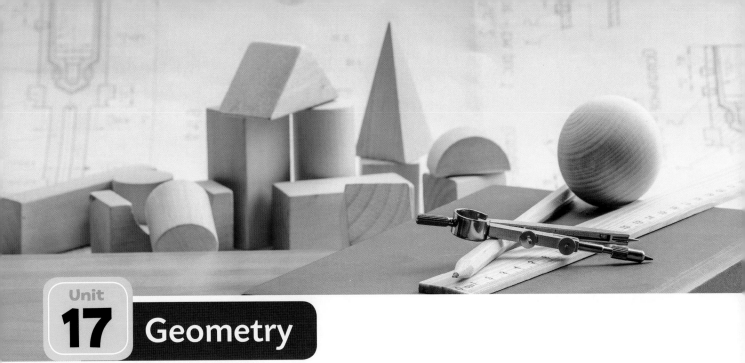

Visual Preview   **What are some common geometric figures?**

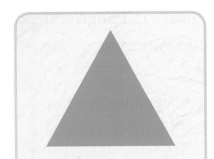

A triangle is
a closed plane figure
that has three sides.

A rectangle is
a parallelogram
with four right angles.

A pentagon is
a closed plane figure
that has five sides.

Vocabulary Preview   **Write the correct word and the meaning in Chinese next to its meaning.**

polygon	proportional	line segment	congruent	parallel

1 _____ : corresponding in size or amount to something else

2 _____ : any closed plane figure with three or more sides

3 _____ : having the exact same size and shape

4 _____ : used to describe lines, paths, etc., that are the same distance apart
along their whole length and do not touch at any point

5 _____ : the finite part of a line lying between any two points on the line

Geometric Figures

17

▲ square

▲ pentagon

Geometry is the study of points, lines, and **angles**. It is also the study of the shapes and figures that can be **constructed** using points, lines, and angles.

A **polygon** is a closed plane figure formed by three or more **line segments**. Polygons are named by the number of sides, angles, or vertices they have.

Polygons with three sides are called triangles. We classify triangles according to the length of their sides and their angles.

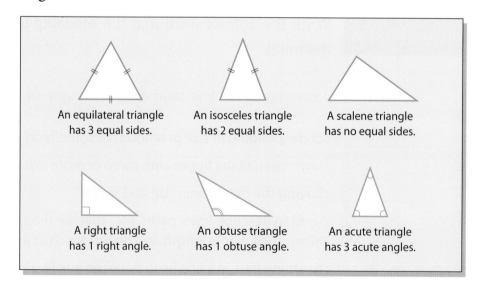

An equilateral triangle has 3 equal sides.	An isosceles triangle has 2 equal sides.	A scalene triangle has no equal sides.
A right triangle has 1 right angle.	An obtuse triangle has 1 obtuse angle.	An acute triangle has 3 acute angles.

Figures that have exactly the same size and shape are **congruent**. Figures that have the same shape, but not the same size, are similar. The lengths of corresponding sides of similar figures are **proportional**.

Four-sided polygons are called **quadrilaterals**. There are five special types of quadrilaterals: parallelograms, rectangles, squares, rhombuses, and trapezoids.

A parallelogram has two pairs of **parallel sides**. The opposite sides and opposite angles are congruent.

A rectangle is a parallelogram in which all the angles are right angles and the opposite sides are the same length. A square has four equal sides and four right angles.

A rhombus is a parallelogram with all four sides congruent. It also has two **axes of symmetry** that run along its diagonals.

A trapezoid also has four sides, but it only has one pair of parallel sides.

A polygon with five sides is a pentagon. One with six sides is a hexagon. A heptagon has seven sides while an octagon has eight. A nonagon has nine sides, and a decagon has ten. In theory, a polygon can have an **unlimited** number of sides. But all of the sides must combine to form a closed figure.

▲ hexagon

▲ octagon

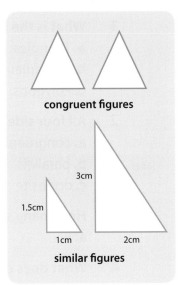

congruent figures

3cm

1.5cm

1cm   2cm

similar figures

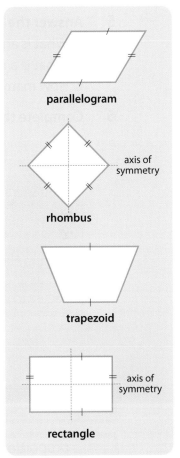

parallelogram

axis of symmetry

rhombus

trapezoid

axis of symmetry

rectangle

Quick Check Check T (True) or F (False).

1 There are two obtuse angles in an obtuse triangle.   T   F
2 There are five types of quadrilaterals.   T   F
3 Figures that have the same size and shape are similar.   T   F

1 **What is the passage mainly about?**
   a. Triangles.
   b. Quadrilaterals.
   c. Polygons.

2 **All four sides of a rhombus are _____ .**
   a. congruent
   b. parallel
   c. opposite

3 **How many sides does a decagon have?**
   a. Six.   **b.** Eight.   **c.** Ten.

4 **What does corresponding mean?**
   a. Opposite.   **b.** Matching.   **c.** Congruent.

5 **Answer the questions.**
   a. What is an equilateral triangle? _____
   b. What is a rhombus? _____
   c. How many sides does a hexagon have? _____

6 **Complete the outline.**

Triangles
• Equilateral triangle = 3 equal sides
• a _____ triangle = 2 equal sides
• b _____ _____ = no equal sides
• Right triangle = 1 right angle
• c _____ _____ = 1 obtuse angle
• Acute triangle = 3 acute angles

Quadrilaterals
• d _____ = 2 pairs of parallel sides
• Rectangle = a parallelogram with 4 right angles
• Square = 4 equal sides + 4 right angles
• Rhombus = a parallelogram with 4 congruent sides
• e _____ = 1 pair of parallel sides

Complete each sentence. Change the form if necessary.

proportional	line segment	parallel side	construct	axis of symmetry

1 A rhombus has two _____ ____ _____ .

2 It takes four _____ _____ to create a rectangle.

3 A rectangle has two _____ _____ since it is a parallelogram.

4 The sides of similar figures are _____ to one another.

5 A right triangle can be _____ with a ruler and a compass.

Who were some of the characters in the *Iliad* and the *Odyssey*?

Helen was the most beautiful woman in the world and the reason why the Trojan War began.

Achilles was the world's greatest warrior, and his only weakness was his heel.

Odysseus had many adventures on his way home after the Trojan War.

Vocabulary Preview **Write the correct word and the meaning in Chinese next to its meaning.**

| kidnap | epic poem | oral | creep | sorceress |

1 _____ : a woman who is a powerful magician

2 _____ : spoken

3 _____ : to take (someone) away illegally by force, typically to obtain a ransom

4 _____ : to move slowly and quietly especially in order to not be noticed

5 _____ : a very long poem about great heroes, monsters, and gods

The *Iliad* and the *Odyssey*

🎧 18

▲ Homer, the greatest poet of ancient Greece

▲ Helen, the most beautiful woman in the world

Around 3,000 years ago, there lived the greatest storyteller in ancient Greece. He was a man named Homer. According to **legend**, Homer was a blind poet. He told two of the greatest stories of all time, the *Iliad* and the *Odyssey*. The *Iliad* and the *Odyssey* are long **epic poems** about great heroes, gods, and goddesses in ancient Greece. Homer was an **oral** poet, so his poems were written down later by people.

The *Iliad* tells about the Trojan War, a long war between the Greeks and the people of Troy. Paris, a prince of Troy, **kidnapped** Helen, the wife of the Greek Menelaus and the most beautiful woman in the world. All of the Greek leaders joined together and attacked Troy. There were many great heroes. They included Ajax, Odysseus, and Agamemnon. But the greatest Greek warrior was Achilles. He was **fearsome** in battle and could not be defeated, except for on his heel, his only weak spot. Meanwhile, the greatest hero defending Troy was Hector.

The Trojan War lasted for ten years. Troy eventually fell because of a clever plan by the Greeks that was **devised by** Odysseus. The Greeks built a giant wooden statue of a horse. They left it outside the walls of the city of Troy and **pretended to** leave. The Trojans brought the horse inside the city because they believed it was an offering to the gods. But there were Greek warriors hiding in the Trojan Horse. That night, the Greek warriors **crept** out of the horse, opened the gates, and captured Troy at last.

▴ the Trojan Horse

▴ **Paris, prince of Troy**

▴ **Achilles' heel**
Paris killed Achilles by shooting him in the heel with a poisoned arrow.

The *Odyssey* tells about the return home of Odysseus. It took Odysseus ten years to reach home after the Trojan War. On his way home to Ithaca, Odysseus had many difficult adventures. He was almost killed by the one-eyed cyclops Polyphemus. He was also almost turned into a pig by the **sorceress** Circe. He visited the underworld, too. He lost his entire crew. However, thanks to the gods—especially Athena—Odysseus returned home and was **greeted by** his faithful wife Penelope.

▴ **Odysseus' return**

▴ **Polyphemus**

Quick Check Check T (True) or F (False).

1 Homer wrote down the *Iliad* and the *Odyssey*. ☐ T ☐ F

2 Agamemnon was the greatest of all the Greek warriors. ☐ T ☐ F

3 Polyphemus was a one-eyed cyclops that almost killed Odysseus. ☐ T ☐ F

1 **What is the passage mainly about?**
  a. The story of Achilles.
  b. Two great epic poems.
  c. The journeys of Odysseus.

2 **The greatest of all the Trojans was _____.**
  a. Hector   **b.** Paris   **c.** Achilles

3 **What did Odysseus encounter on his journey home?**
  a. The Trojan Horse.
  b. The wrath of Achilles.
  c. The sorceress Circe.

4 **What does offering mean?**
  a. Meeting.   **b.** Sacrifice.   **c.** Prayer.

5 **Complete the sentences.**
  a. Helen's husband was the Greek _____.
  b. The Trojan Horse was a great statue made of _____.
  c. Odysseus visited the _____ on his way home to Ithaca.

6 **Complete the outline.**

The *Iliad*
- Tells about the ᵃ_____ _____
- Helen was kidnapped by Paris.
- The Greeks joined to attack the Trojans for ten years.
- The Greeks used the ᵇ_____ _____ to defeat the Trojans.

The *Odyssey*
- Tells about the return home of ᶜ_____
- Took him ten years to reach home
- Odysseus was almost killed by a ᵈ_____
- Encountered the sorceress Circe
- Visited the underworld
- Lost his crew
- Was greeted by his wife Penelope when he arrived home

Complete each sentence. Change the form if necessary.

| kidnap | devised by | pretend to | creep out of | greeted by |

1 Paris _____ Helen and took her to Troy to be his wife.

2 The Greeks _____ _____ leave Troy, but they really hid from the Trojans.

3 At first, the Trojan Horse was _____ _____ the Trojans with happiness.

4 Odysseus and his men _____ _____ _____ the cyclops' cave to avoid being eaten.

5 Many brilliant ideas, like the Trojan Horse, were _____ _____ Odysseus.

Learning About Language

What are some different figures of speech?

"Juliet is the sun" is an example of a metaphor.

"The wind is whispering" is an example of personification.

The buzzing bee and hissing snake are examples of onomatopoeia.

Write the correct word and the meaning in Chinese next to its meaning.

metaphor	literally	simile	onomatopoeia	personification

1 _____ : the use of words that sound like the sound which they refer to

2 _____ : a comparison that uses "like" or "as"

3 _____ : giving an animal or a thing human characteristics

4 _____ : a comparison between two things that seem to have no connection

5 _____ : in the most basic, obvious meanings of the words that are used

Figures of Speech

🎧 19

simile

He roared like a lion.

She was as meek as a lamb.

When writers create literature, they use both literal and **figurative language**. **Literal language** says exactly what you mean. Much writing uses literal language. However, many writers **employ** figurative language as well. This makes their writing much more creative. It also gives their writing more imagination. There are many different ways for writers to use figurative language.

One way is to use figures of speech. A **figure of speech** is an expression that is not meant to be taken **literally**. These often create images in the readers' minds. **Similes** and **metaphors** are two of the most popular figures of speech. Both are comparisons. However, similes are direct comparisons while metaphors are indirect comparisons.

In addition, similes often use "as" or "like" to compare two things. For instance, one simile is "Love is like a rose." Many similes refer to animals. "He roared like a lion" and "She was as meek as a lamb" are two more similes. Metaphors are

90

metaphor

He is a mule.

▲ a sea of sand

not **as obvious as** similes. Metaphors compare two unlike things that seem to have nothing in common. And they do not use "like" or "as." "She is the apple of my eye," "He is a mule," and "There is a sea of sand" are examples of metaphors.

Another common figure of speech is **personification**. This is the giving of human characteristics to animals, plants, things, or ideas. "The moon is sleeping," "The walls have ears," and "Time waits for no one" are examples of personification.

Some writers like to use **onomatopoeia** in their works. This is using words that sound like the things that they describe. For instance, a snake might "hiss," a bee might "buzz," and a bell might go "ding dong."

onomatopoeia

Buzzzzz...

Bees buzz.

Oink Oink

Pigs oink.

Hisssss...

Snakes hiss.

Ding dong

Bells go "ding dong."

personification

The moon is sleeping.   The walls have ears.

Quick Check   Check T (True) or F (False).

1   Figurative language should be taken literally.   ☐ T   ☐ F

2   Personification can be used when talking about animals.   ☐ T   ☐ F

3   Onomatopoeia is a comparison between two different animals.   ☐ T   ☐ F

1 **What is the main idea of the passage?**
    a. Writers can use language in many different ways.
    b. Most writers prefer literal language to figurative language.
    c. Metaphors and similes are the most common figures of speech.

2 **"He roared like a lion" is a _____.**
    a. simile   **b.** metaphor   **c.** personification

3 **What is personification?**
    a. It is the making of a comparison using "as" or "like."
    b. It is the writing of words that sound like they are written.
    c. It is the giving of human characteristics to animals or things.

4 **What does meek mean?**
    a. Brave.   **b.** Strong.   **c.** Gentle.

5 **According to the passage, which statement is true?**
    a. A simile is a comparison between two unlike things.
    b. There are many types of figures of speech in English.
    c. Personification is a kind of literal language.

6 **Complete the outline.**

Comparisons

Simile
- Is a comparison that uses "like" or "as"
- Often refers to ᵃ_____
  ᵇ_____
- Is a comparison that is not as obvious as a simile
- Is between two ᶜ_____ things
- Does not use "like" or "as"

Other Figures of Speech

Personification
- Is the giving of ᵈ_____ characteristics to animals, plants, things, or ideas
  ᵉ_____
- Is the using of words that sound like the things that they describe

Complete each sentence. Change the form if necessary.

literal language	literally	as obvious as	onomatopoeia	employ

1 Some examples of _____ are quack, moo, and baa.

2 Metaphors are not _____ similes are when used as comparisons.

3 Writers of nonfiction often use _____ _____.

4 Some writers like to _____ metaphors in their works.

5 Do not take a simile _____; it is a figure of speech.

What are some features of Classical Art?

Classical Art focused on simplicity and proportion.

Columns were frequently used in Greek and Roman architecture.

Many statues from ancient Greece and Rome stressed the harmonious form of the human body.

Write the correct word and the meaning in Chinese next to its meaning.

proportion	Doric order	Ionic order	symmetrical	depict

1 _____ : the style of columns that had spiral scrolls on the capitals

2 _____ : the simplest in style of all columns

3 _____ : having sides or halves that are the same

4 _____ : to describe someone or something using words or pictures

5 _____ : a comparative relation in size, number, or quantity

Greek and Roman Art

🎧20

In art history, Classical Art has been a very **influential** period of art to many later eras. Classical Art refers to art from ancient Greece and Rome. The ancient Greeks and Romans created many wonderful works of art, including pottery, sculptures, and buildings.

Classical Art **focused on** simplicity and **proportion**. The ancient Greeks led the way. They considered balance and proportion to be the most important qualities in art. One of the easiest ways to understand Classical Art is to look at the architecture of this period.

When the ancient Greeks built buildings, they used **columns** as supports and followed one of three classical orders: Doric, Ionic, and Corinthian. Most

Column Style

Doric order   Ionic order   Corinthian order

94

columns have a base at the bottom, a shaft in the middle, and a capital at the top. The **Doric order** was the oldest and simplest in style and usually had no base. The **Ionic order** had capitals decorated with spiral scrolls. And the **Corinthian order** had the most decorated and elaborate capitals.

▲ the Parthenon

The Romans were **admirers** of Greek art and created copies of many Greek works. But they also introduced some new elements from the Egyptians.

In Greece, the Temple of Apollo, the Temple of Hera, and the Parthenon are examples of Classical architecture. In Rome, the Coliseum and the Pantheon are two examples. The buildings are all **symmetrical** and are fine examples of the classical emphasis on balance and proportion.

▲ the Temple of Apollo

The ancient Greeks and Romans also created many beautiful sculptures. They focused on the beauty of nature and the harmony of the human body. They **depicted** the human body as a well-proportioned and harmonious form. Myron's *Discus Thrower* and *Apollo Belvedere* are fine examples that show the beauty and proportion of the human body.

▲ the Coliseum

▲ the Pantheon

▲ *Apollo Belvedere*

Quick Check Check T (True) or F (False).

1 There were three major orders of columns in Classical Art. T F
2 The Temple of Hera is an example of architecture from ancient Rome. T F
3 The Greeks and Romans were interested in proportion when making sculptures. T F

1 **What is the passage mainly about?**

    a. How Classical Art affected later periods.

    b. The styles used in Classical Art.

    c. Some famous examples of Classical Art.

2 **A Roman example of Classical architecture is _____.**

    a. the Parthenon   **b.** the Temple of Apollo   **c.** the Pantheon

3 **What was unique about the Doric order of columns?**

    a. The columns were highly decorated.

    b. The columns often did not have a base.

    c. The columns had capitals with spiral scrolls.

4 **What does elaborate mean?**

    a. Detailed.   **b.** Expensive.   **c.** Proportional.

5 **Answer the questions.**

    a. What did Classical Art focus on? _____

    b. What were the three main orders of columns? _____

    c. How did the ancient Greeks and Romans depict the human body?

    _____

6 **Complete the outline.**

Classical Art
• Refers to art from ancient ^a_____ and Rome
• Focused on ^b_____ and proportion
• Stressed the beauty of nature and the harmony of the human body

Classical Architecture
• Used ^c_____ as supports
• Doric order = simple with no base
• Ionic order = capitals decorated with ^d_____ _____
• Corinthian order = most decorated and elaborate ^e_____
• Made symmetrical buildings emphasized balance and proportion

influential   focus on   column   symmetrical   depict

1 Roman sculptors _____ _____ beauty and proportion when making statues.

2 The Greeks used _____ to help support their buildings.

3 Many classical sculptures _____ great heroes or gods.

4 The orders of columns were all very _____ during ancient times.

5 The majority of classical buildings were designed to be _____.

Classical Music

Who are some famous classical music composers?

George Frederic Handel was
one of the greatest composers
of the Baroque Period.

Wolfgang Amadeus Mozart
was a child genius from
the Classical Period.

Franz Schubert was one of
the most famous composers
of the Romantic Period.

Vocabulary Preview Write the correct word and the meaning in Chinese next to its meaning.

compose	Baroque Period	piece	Classical Period	passionate

1 _____ : a song or some kind of written music

2 _____ : a period known for its lively and complicated music

3 _____ : showing or expressing strong beliefs, interest, or enthusiasm

4 _____ : to write a piece of music

5 _____ : a period known for its lighter and less complicated music

The Western Musical Tradition

🎧 21

▲ **Bach**

▲ **Handel**

Throughout history, there have been many periods of music. Among the most famous are the Baroque, Classical, and Romantic periods. The **composers** who lived during these periods wrote some of the greatest of all classical music.

The **Baroque Period** lasted from around 1600 to 1750. Two of its greatest composers were Johann Sebastian Bach and George Frederic Handel. Many new forms of music, such as **operas**, oratorios, and passions, were created in the Baroque Period. There was often an emphasis on religious music. Both Bach and Handel are well known for their music with religious themes. Bach **composed** *St. Matthew Passion*. Handel wrote *The Messiah*, which contains the *Hallelujah Chorus*. Baroque music was often complicated and difficult to play. It was also known for its liveliness. Handel's *Water Music* and *Royal Fireworks Music* are **representative pieces** from that age.

The next great age was the **Classical Period**. It lasted from around 1750 to 1825. Wolfgang Amadeus Mozart, Joseph Haydn, and Ludwig van Beethoven are the three greatest composers from this era. All three men were born in Vienna, Austria, so Vienna became the **focal point** of this period. Classical music was both lighter and less complicated than Baroque. Unlike Baroque music, the mood in a piece of classical music often changed, and the pieces were shorter as well. Sonatas and symphonies were popular then. Beethoven's *Ninth Symphony*, Mozart's *The Marriage of Figaro*, and Haydn's *Surprise Symphony* are some popular works from that period.

▲ Mozart

The **Romantic Period** lasted from around 1815 to 1910. The works then often expressed strong emotions, making them **passionate**. Fantasy and imagination were key aspects for the composers when they were writing their music. More instruments were added to the orchestras than were used during the Classical Period. Many works in this period, like those of Richard Wagner, were quite long. Among the famous composers of the Romantic Period were Franz Schubert, Robert Schumann, and Frédéric Chopin.

▲ Haydn

▲ Beethoven

Romantic Period

▲ Shubert

▲ Schumann

▲ Chopin

Quick Check Check T (True) or F (False).

1 Bach and Handel composed during the Classical Period.　T　F
2 Haydn was the composer of the *Surprise Symphony*.　T　F
3 Many works during the Romantic Period were very long.　T　F

1 **What is the main idea of the passage?**
   a. Bach, Mozart, and Beethoven were three great composers.
   b. The Baroque Period was the first of the major periods of music.
   c. There have been many influential periods of classical music.

2 **Vienna, Austria, was an important city during the _____.**
   a. Baroque Period   **b.** Classical Period   **c.** Romantic Period

3 **What was a feature of the Classical Period?**
   a. The mood in a piece of music could often change.
   b. The music was complicated for the musicians to play.
   c. Fantasy was an important element of the music.

4 **What does liveliness mean?**
   a. Energy.   **b.** Creativity.   **c.** Length.

5 **Complete the sentences.**
   a. _____ and Handel were two major composers from the Baroque Period.
   b. Sonatas and _____ were popular during the Classical Period.
   c. Orchestras in the Romantic Period added several _____.

6 **Complete the outline.**

Baroque Period	Classical Period	Romantic Period
• ᵃ_____ and Handel • Used new forms of music • Was much ᵇ_____ music • Music was complicated and difficult to play.	• Mozart, Haydn, and ᶜ_____ • Was lighter and less complicated music • Mood changes in short pieces. • Sonatas and ᵈ_____ were popular.	• Schubert, Schumann, and ᵉ_____ • Strong, passionate works • Added new instruments to orchestras • Wrote long works

Complete each sentence. Change the form if necessary.

| opera   compose   representative   focal point   passionate |

1 Some people were able to _____ new music quickly.

2 One _____ of the Baroque Period was religious music.

3 A musical piece that tells a story through singing and acting is an _____.

4 Beethoven is a _____ composer of the Classical Period.

5 The pieces written by many Romantic Period composers are very _____.

A

Complete each sentence with the correct word. Change the form if necessary.

pretend to	represent	decimal system	almost	Arabic numeral
proportional	creep out of	odd number	categorize	axis of symmetry

1   The numerals we use today are called _____ _____.

2   Roman numerals were symbols that were used to _____ numbers.

3   All integers can be _____ as positive or negative.

4   The _____ _____ is based on the number ten.

5   Numbers such as 1, 3, 5, 7, or 9 are _____ _____.

6   A rhombus has two _____ _____ _____.

7   The sides of similar figures are _____ to one another.

8   The Greek warriors _____ _____ leave Troy, but they really were hiding in the Trojan horse.

9   The Greek warriors _____ _____ _____ the horse and captured Troy at last.

10   Odysseus was _____ killed by the one-eyed cyclops Polyphemus.

B

Complete each sentence with the correct word. Change the form if necessary.

focus on	literally	comparison	influential	literal language
focal point	Ionic	Corinthian	admirer	personification

1   _____ _____ says exactly what you mean.

2   A figure of speech is an expression that is not meant to be taken _____.

3   Similes are stated _____ while metaphors are indirect comparisons.

4   _____ is the giving of human characteristics to animals, plants, things, or ideas.

5   Classical Art has been a very _____ period of art to many later eras.

6   Classical Art _____ _____ simplicity and proportion.

7   The _____ order had capitals decorated with spiral scrolls.

8   The _____ order had the most decorated and elaborate capitals.

9   The Romans were _____ of Greek art and created copies of many Greek works.

10   One _____ _____ of the Baroque Period was religious music.

C

Match each word with the correct definition and write the meaning in Chinese.

1 integer _____ ☐

2 complicated _____ ☐

3 geometry _____ ☐

4 congruent _____ ☐

5 quadrilateral _____ ☐

6 figurative language _____ ☐

7 metaphor _____ ☐

8 sorceress _____ ☐

9 oral _____ ☐

10 epic poem _____ ☐

a. spoken

b. a polygon with four sides

c. difficult to understand or deal with

d. the study of points, lines, and angles

e. a woman who is a powerful magician

f. having the exact same size and shape

g. more creative language than literal language

h. a number that is neither a fraction nor a decimal

i. a very long poem about great heroes, monsters, and gods

j. a comparison between two things that seem to have no connection

D

Write the meanings of the words in Chinese.

1 decimal system _____

2 be greeted by _____

3 creep out of _____

4 be devised by _____

5 positive integer _____

6 polygon _____

7 unlimited _____

8 legend _____

9 fearsome _____

10 onomatopoeia _____

11 as obvious as _____

12 employ _____

13 literally _____

14 column _____

15 influential _____

16 symmetrical _____

17 representative _____

18 passionate _____

19 simile _____

20 personification _____

21 figure of speech _____

22 Ionic order _____

23 Doric order _____

24 Corinthian order _____

25 admirer _____

26 proportion _____

27 Baroque Period _____

28 Romantic Period _____

29 Classical Period _____

30 focal point _____

● Word List
● Answers and Translations

Word List

01 The U.S. Geography— The Regions of the United States

1	**geographic** (a.)	地理的
2	**physical environment**	自然環境
3	**set . . . apart**	將……分開
4	**District of Columbia**	哥倫比亞特區
5	**Atlantic Coastal Plain**	大西洋沿岸平原
6	**mountain range**	山脈
7	**subregion** (n.)	子區域
8	**be known for**	以……而聞名
9	**Pilgrim** (n.)	西元1620年搭乘五月花號（*Mayflower*）移居美洲的英國清教徒
10	**Puritan** (n.)	清教徒
11	**densely populated**	人口密度高的
12	**urban** (a.)	城市的
13	**metropolitan** (a.)	大都市的
14	**growing season**	生長季
15	**cash crop**	經濟作物
16	**plantation** (n.)	大農場
17	**prairie** (n.)	大草原；牧場
18	**stretch** (v.)	延伸
19	**as far as the eye can see**	視線所及
20	**the Great Lakes**	北美五大湖
21	**fertile** (a.)	肥沃的
22	**cropland** (n.)	農田
23	**agriculture** (n.)	農業
24	**breadbasket** (n.)	產糧區；麵包籃
25	**arid** (a.)	乾燥的
26	**numerous** (a.)	為數眾多的
27	**diverse** (a.)	多樣的
28	**dominate** (v.)	高聳於；俯視

02 The United States— A Nation of Diversity

1	**a nation of immigrants**	移民國家
2	**race** (n.)	種族
3	**century** (n.)	世紀
4	**a multicultural society**	多元文化社會
5	**at the same time**	同時
6	**immigration** (n.)	移民
7	**in various stages**	在不同的階段
8	**against one's will**	違背某人的意願
9	**pour into**	湧入
10	**newcomer** (n.)	新來的人
11	**stream into**	流入
12	**spread out**	散布
13	**concentrate in**	集中在某處
14	**Jewish** (a.)	猶太人的
15	**ethnic group**	族群
16	**nationality** (n.)	國籍
17	**get along with**	與……和睦相處
18	**encounter** (v.)	遭受
19	**discrimination** (n.)	歧視
20	**treat** (v.)	對待
21	**fairly** (adv.)	公平地
22	**no matter what**	無論什麼
23	**in harmony**	和諧

03 The U.S. Economy— From Farming to Technology

1	**distribute** (v.)	分發；分銷
2	**producer** (n.)	生產者
3	**consumer** (n.)	消費者
4	**economy** (n.)	經濟
5	**gross domestic product (GDP)**	國內生產總值；國內生產毛額
6	**be based on**	根基於
7	**majority** (n.)	大多數

8	colonist (n.)	殖民地開拓者；殖民地居民	14	surroundings (n.)	環境
9	manufacturing industry	製造業	15	wander (v.)	流浪；漫遊
10	finance industry	金融業	16	teepee (n.)	梯皮（美國印第安人的圓錐形帳篷）
11	technology industry	科技業	17	cone-shaped (a.)	圓錐形的
12	fastest-growing (a.)	發展最迅速的	18	harsh (a.)	嚴酷的
13	free market economy	自由市場經濟	19	dry farming	旱作
14	manufacture (v.)	製造	20	out of	用……作材料
15	storeowner (n.)	商店老闆	21	adobe (n.)	曬乾的泥磚
16	consider (v.)	考慮	22	extreme (a.)	極端的
17	opportunity cost	機會成本	23	whale (n.)	鯨
18	make a decision	做決定	24	craft worker	工藝工作者
19	interference (n.)	干涉	25	totem pole	圖騰柱
20	free-enterprise system	自由企業制度	26	canoe (n.)	獨木舟
21	run one's own business	經營某人自己的事業	27	crafts (n.)	工藝品（多用複數形）
22	entrepreneur (n.)	企業家；創業者	28	alliance (n.)	同盟；結盟
23	in most cases	大多數情況下	29	Iroquois Confederacy	易洛魁聯盟
24	law of supply and demand	供需法則	30	deal with	與……交易
25	go down	下降			
26	scarce (a.)	缺乏的			

05 The European Exploration of Asia and the Americas—The Age of Exploration

04 People and Culture— The Native People of North America

1	native people	原住民	1	fifteenth century	十五世紀
2	archaeologist (n.)	考古學家	2	spice (n.)	香料
3	land bridge	陸橋	3	in great demand	需求量大
4	strip of land	狹長陸地	4	be willing to	樂意；願意
5	herd (n.)	畜群	5	pay high price	付高價
6	hunting trip	狩獵旅行	6	merchant (n.)	商人
7	gather (v.)	採集	7	by land	由陸路
8	hunter-gatherer (n.)	採獵者	8	search for	尋找
9	ancestor (n.)	祖先	9	route (n.)	路線
10	Native American	美洲原住民	10	compete to	爭相做某事
11	civilization (n.)	文明	11	sea route	海路
12	tribe (n.)	部落	12	lead the way	領路；打先鋒
13	adapt (v.)	適應	13	Portuguese (n.) (a.)	葡萄牙人；葡萄牙的
			14	caravel (n.)	卡拉維爾帆船；輕快帆船
			15	farther (adv.)	更遠地

16	**Prince Henry the Navigator**	航海家亨利王子
17	**expedition** (n.)	探險隊；遠征隊
18	**steadily** (adv.)	平穩地
19	**round** (v.)	繞行
20	**southern tip of Africa**	非洲南端
21	**Cape of Good Hope**	好望角
22	**waterway** (n.)	水路
23	**convince** (v.)	說服
24	**sponsor** (v.)	資助
25	**mission** (n.)	任務
26	**set sail**	啟航
27	**circumnavigation** (n.)	環球航行
28	**soon afterward**	不久之後
29	**the Age of Exploration**	大航海時代
30	**the Age of Discovery**	地理大發現

18	**gun** (n.)	槍
19	**cannon** (n.)	火砲
20	**metal armor**	盔甲
21	**ride a horse**	騎馬
22	**deadly** (a.)	致命的
23	**disease** (n.)	疾病
24	**horrible** (a.)	可怕的
25	**smallpox** (n.)	天花
26	**immunity** (n.)	免疫力
27	**defeat** (v.)	擊敗
28	**enslave** (v.)	奴役
29	**claim** (v.)	聲稱
30	**set up**	建立

06 Europeans in the Americas— The Spanish Conquerors in the Americas

1	**Spaniard** (n.)	西班牙人
2	**in search of**	尋找
3	**proceed to**	開始；著手
4	**ignore** (v.)	忽視
5	**right** (n.)	權利
6	**local people**	當地居民
7	**modern-day** (a.)	今日的
8	**riches** (n.)	財富
9	**establish** (v.)	建立
10	**colony** (n.)	殖民地
11	**conquer** (v.)	征服
12	**conquistador** (n.)	征服者
13	**capture** (v.)	捕捉
14	**end** (v.)	結束
15	**decade** (n.)	十年
16	**fierce** (a.)	兇猛的
17	**weapon** (n.)	武器

07 Colonial America— The First French and English Colonies

1	**focus on**	集中於
2	**colonize** (v.)	將……開拓為殖民地
3	**interior** (n.)	內部
4	**permanent** (a.)	永久的
5	**settlement** (n.)	殖民地
6	**settle in**	定居於
7	**be founded at**	建立於
8	**seek** (v.)	尋找
9	**fortune** (n.)	財富
10	**get rich**	致富
11	**thanks to**	幸虧
12	**Indian chief**	印地安酋長
13	**prosper** (v.)	繁榮
14	**Pilgrim**	西元1620年搭乘五月花號（*Mayflower*）移居美洲的英國清教徒
15	**belief** (n.)	信仰
16	**Puritan** (n.)	清教徒
17	**deeply** (adv.)	強烈地
18	**religious** (a.)	宗教的

19	**Christian** (n.)	基督徒
20	**Holland** (n.)	荷蘭
21	**eventually** (adv.)	最後；終於
22	**separate** (a.)	獨立的

26	**Declaration of Independence**	《獨立宣言》
27	**proclaim** (v.)	宣告
28	**appoint** (v.)	指派
29	**Continental Army**	大陸軍
30	**surrender** (v.) (n.)	投降

08　The Declaration of Independence— The American Revolution

1	**1760s** (n.)	1760年代
2	**be ruled by**	被……統治
3	**meanwhile** (adv.)	其間
4	**Seven Year's War**	七年戰爭
5	**pay off**	清償
6	**debt** (n.)	債
7	**tax** (v.)	向……課稅
8	**Parliament** (n.)	英國國會
9	**Sugar Act**	《糖稅法》
10	**Stamp Act**	《印花稅法》
11	**extra** (a.)	額外的
12	**protest** (v.)	抗議
13	**Intolerable Acts**	不可容忍法令
14	**boycott** (v.)	聯合抵制；杯葛
15	**taxation** (n.)	課稅
16	**representation** (n.)	代表
17	**representative** (n.)	代表人
18	**refuse** (v.)	拒絕
19	**independence** (n.)	獨立
20	**tension** (n.)	緊張局勢
21	**minuteman** (n.)	（美國獨立戰爭期間）命令一下立即應召的民兵 *pl.* minutemen
22	**notice** (n.)	通知
23	**redcoat** (n.)	（美國獨立戰爭時期的）英國軍人，因穿紅制服而得其名。
24	**Revolutionary War**	（美國）獨立戰爭
25	**Continental Congress**	大陸會議

09　How Are Living Things Classified?— The Five Kingdoms of Organisms

1	**be classified by**	根據……分類
2	**in common**	共同的
3	**kingdom** (n.)	（生物分類上的）界
4	**Monera Kingdom**	原核生物界
5	**Protista Kingdom**	原生生物界
6	**Fungi Kingdom**	真菌界
7	**Plantae Kingdom**	植物界
8	**Animalia Kingdom**	動物界
9	**single-celled** (a.)	單細胞的
10	**prokaryote** (n.)	原核生物
11	**lack** (v.)	缺少
12	**nucleus** (n.)	細胞核
13	**animallike** (a.)	似動物的
14	**algae** (n.)	alga 的複數形 水藻；海藻（常用複數）
15	**plantlike** (a.)	似植物的
16	**microscopic** (a.)	只能從顯微鏡裡看到的；微小的
17	**amoeba** (n.)	阿米巴；變形蟲
18	**chloroplast** (n.)	葉綠體
19	**enable** (v.)	使能夠
20	**photosynthesis** (n.)	光合作用
21	**multi-celled** (a.)	多細胞的
22	**mold** (n.)	黴菌
23	**yeast** (n.)	酵母（菌）
24	**mushroom** (n.)	蘑菇；傘菌
25	**feed on**	以……為食物
26	**decay** (v.)	腐爛

27	**multicellular** (a.)	多細胞的
28	**fern** (n.)	蕨類植物
29	**moss** (n.)	苔蘚植物
30	**chlorophyll** (n.)	葉綠素

10 **Classification—
The Seven Levels of Classification**

1	**name** (v.) (n.)	命名；名稱
2	**take care of**	處理
3	**Latin** (a.)	拉丁語的
4	**Linnaean System**	林奈分類系統
5	**basis** (n.)	根據
6	**level** (n.)	級別
7	**kingdom** (n.)	（生物分類上的）界
8	**phylum** (n.)	（生物分類上的）門
9	**class** (n.)	（生物分類上的）綱
10	**order** (n.)	（生物分類上的）目
11	**family** (n.)	（生物分類上的）科
12	**genus** (n.)	（生物分類上的）屬
13	**species** (n.)	（生物分類上的）種
14	**particular** (a.)	特有的
15	**specific** (a.)	明確的
16	**body plan**	體型呈現
17	**Chordata** (n.)	脊索動物門
18	**backbone** (n.)	脊骨
19	**carnivore** (n.)	肉食性動物
20	**herbivore** (n.)	草食性動物
21	**related** (a.)	相關的
22	**precise** (a.)	精確的
23	**specify** (v.)	明確說明
24	**typically** (adv.)	通常；一般
25	**human being**	人類
26	*Homo sapiens*	智人

11 **How Plants Meet Their Needs—
Plant Structures and Functions**

1	**basic need**	基本需要
2	**part** (n.)	部分；部位；構造
3	**function** (n.)	功能
4	**hold** (v.)	托住；支撐
5	**anchor** (v.)	使固定
6	**prevent ... from ...**	防止……
7	**be responsible for**	負責
8	**structure** (n.)	構造
9	**tiny** (a.)	微小的
10	**root hair**	根毛
11	**cortex**	皮層
12	**xylem** (n.)	木質部
13	**transportation system**	運輸系統
14	**phloem** (n.)	韌皮部
15	**underground stem**	地下莖
16	**cactus** (n.)	仙人掌 （複數為 cacti/cactuses）
17	**undergo** (v.)	進行
18	**process** (n.)	過程
19	**carbon dioxide**	二氧化碳
20	**sugar** (n.)	糖
21	**oxygen** (n.)	氧氣
22	**release** (v.)	釋放
23	**breathe** (v.)	呼吸
24	**respiration** (n.)	呼吸（作用）

12 **How Do Plants Reproduce?—
Flowers and Seeds**

1	**seed** (n.)	種子
2	**reproductive organ**	生殖器官
3	**male part**	雄性構造
4	**female part**	雌性構造
5	**pollen** (n.)	花粉
6	**stamen** (n.)	雄蕊

7	anther (n.)	花藥
8	filament (n.)	花絲
9	stalk (n.)	柄
10	pistil (n.)	雌蕊
11	stigma (n.)	柱頭
12	style (n.)	花柱
13	ovary (n.)	子房
14	be fertilized	受精
15	be pollinated	被授花粉
16	pollination (n.)	授粉（作用）
17	be transferred	被轉移
18	self-pollination (n.)	自花授粉
19	cross-pollination (n.)	異花授粉
20	petal (n.)	花瓣
21	outer covering	外層覆蓋物
22	get stuck on	黏在……上
23	pollen tube	花粉管
24	fertilization (n.)	受精（作用）
25	embryo (n.)	胚芽
26	germinate (v.)	發芽

13 What Are Some Types of Plants?— Plants With Seeds

1	majority (n.)	大多數
2	seed plant	種子植物
3	angiosperm (n.)	被子植物
4	gymnosperm (n.)	裸子植物
5	flowering plant	開花植物
6	be based on	根據
7	seed leaf	子葉
8	monocotyledon (n.)	單子葉植物
9	cotyledon (n.)	子葉
10	dicotyledon (n.)	雙子葉植物
11	cone (n.)	毬果
12	evergreen (n.)	常綠樹
13	needlelike (a.)	針狀的

14	conifer (n.)	松柏科植物；針葉樹
15	cedar (n.)	西洋杉
16	cypress (n.)	柏樹
17	cycad (n.)	蘇鐵
18	gingko (n.)	銀杏
19	mature (v.)	成熟
20	scatter (v.)	使分散
21	carry away	帶走
22	dominant (a.)	主要的

14 Plants Without Seeds— Seedless Vascular Plants and Nonvascular Plants

1	reproduce (v.)	繁殖
2	seedless (a.)	無種子的
3	vascular plant	維管束植物
4	nonvascular plant	非維管束植物
5	vascular tissue	維管束組織
6	tubelike (a.)	管狀的
7	common (a.)	普遍的；常見的
8	vein (n.)	葉脈
9	fern (n.)	蕨類植物
10	thrive (v.)	茂盛生長
11	frond (n.)	蕨葉
12	rhizome (n.)	地下莖
13	spore (n.)	孢子
14	alike (a.)	相像的
15	separate (a.)	獨立的
16	stage (n.)	階段
17	asexually (adv.)	無性地；無性生殖地
18	spore case	孢子囊
19	damp (a.)	潮濕的
20	asexual reproduction	無性生殖
21	sperm (cell) (n.)	精子（細胞）
22	egg (cell) (n.)	卵子（細胞）
23	fertilized egg	受精卵
24	sexual reproduction	有性生殖

15 Plant Responses and Adaptations—How Do Plants Respond to Their Environments?

1	**adaptation** (n.)	適應
2	**respond to**	對……做出反應
3	**tend to**	傾向
4	**tropism** (n.)	向性
5	**response** (n.)	反應
6	**external** (a.)	外部的
7	**stimulus** (n.)	刺激
8	**phototropism** (n.)	向光性
9	**bend** (v.)	彎曲
10	**toward** (prep.)	朝向
11	**gravitropism** (n.)	向地性
12	**gravity** (n.)	重力
13	**downward** (adv.)	向下
14	**while** (conj.)	而
15	**hydrotropism** (n.)	向水性
16	**source of water**	水源
17	**involuntary** (a.)	非自主性的
18	**endure** (v.)	忍受
19	**store** (v.)	貯藏
20	**carnivorous** (a.)	肉食性的
21	**Venus flytrap**	捕蠅草
22	**sustain** (v.)	供養

16 Numbers and Number Sense—Understanding Numbers

1	**Arabic numeral**	阿拉伯數字
2	**digit** (n.)	數字
3	**decimal system**	十進制
4	**encounter** (v.)	遇到
5	**Roman numeral**	羅馬數字
6	**represent** (v.)	代表
7	**numerical value**	數值
8	**rule** (n.)	規則

9	**repeat** (v.)	重複
10	**subtract** (v.)	減去
11	**extremely** (adv.)	非常地；極端地
12	**complicated** (a.)	複雜的
13	**imagine** (v.)	想像
14	**fortunately** (adv.)	幸運地
15	**positive** (a.)	正的
16	**negative** (a.)	負的
17	**number line**	數線
18	**neither ... nor ...**	既非……也非……
19	**whole number**	整數
20	**integer** (n.)	整數
21	**decimal** (n.)	小數
22	**fraction** (n.)	分數
23	**mixed number**	帶分數
24	**positive integer**	正整數
25	**negative integer**	負整數
26	**even number**	偶數
27	**odd number**	奇數
28	**end in**	以……結尾

17 Geometry—Geometric Figures

1	**geometry** (n.)	幾何學
2	**construct** (v.)	作圖；畫
3	**polygon** (n.)	多邊形
4	**closed figure**	封閉圖形
5	**plane figure**	平面圖形
6	**vertex** (n.)	頂點
7	**equilateral triangle**	等邊三角形
8	**isosceles triangle**	等腰三角形
9	**scalene triangle**	不等邊三角形；不規則三角形
10	**congruent** (a.)	全等的
11	**corresponding side**	對應邊
12	**similar figure**	相似圖形

13	proportional (a.)	成比例的
14	quadrilateral (n.)	四邊形
15	parallelogram (n.)	平行四邊形
16	rhombus (n.)	菱形
17	trapezoid (n.)	梯形
18	parallel (a.)	平行的
19	axis of symmetry	對稱軸（axis 之複數為 axes）
20	diagonal (a.)	對角線的
21	pentagon (n.)	五邊形
22	hexagon (n.)	六邊形
23	heptagon (n.)	七邊形
24	octagon (n.)	八邊形
25	nonagon (n.)	九邊形
26	decagon (n.)	十邊形
27	in theory	理論上
28	unlimited (a.)	無限的

18 Myths and Legends — The Iliad and the Odyssey

1	storyteller (n.)	講故事的人
2	legend (n.)	傳說
3	blind (a.)	盲的
4	Iliad (n.)	伊里亞德
5	Odyssey (n.)	奧德賽
6	epic poem	史詩
7	oral (a.)	口述的
8	be written down	被記載下來
9	Trojan War	特洛伊戰爭
10	kidnap (v.)	綁架；劫持
11	Menelaus (n.)	墨涅拉俄斯
12	attack (v.)	攻擊
13	Ajax (n.)	阿傑克斯
14	Odysseus (n.)	奧德修斯
15	Agamemnon (n.)	阿卡曼農
16	Achilles (n.)	阿基里斯

17	fearsome (a.)	令人生畏的
18	heel (n.)	腳後跟
19	weak spot	弱點
20	defend (v.)	保衛
21	Hector (n.)	赫克特
22	be devised by	由……設計
23	pretend to	假裝
24	offering (n.)	禮物；供品
25	creep out of	自……爬出
26	on one's way	在途中
27	almost (adv.)	差點
28	cyclops (n.)	獨眼巨人（複數為 cyclopes）
29	sorceress (n.)	女巫
30	be greeted by	被……迎接

19 Learning About Language— Figures of Speech

1	literature (n.)	文學；文學作品
2	literal language	字面性語言
3	figurative language	比喻性語言
4	employ (v.)	使用
5	creative (a.)	富創造力的
6	imagination (n.)	想像力
7	figure of speech	修辭（手法）
8	literally (adv.)	照字面地
9	reader (n.)	讀者
10	mind (n.)	心
11	simile (n.)	明喻
12	metaphor (n.)	隱喻
13	popular (a.)	普遍的
14	comparison (n.)	比喻；比較
15	direct (a.)	直接
16	indirect (a.)	間接
17	refer to	涉及；關於
18	meek (a.)	溫順的

19	**lamb** (n.)	小羊
20	**as obvious as**	像……一樣明顯
21	**in common**	共同的
22	**mule** (n.)	騾
23	**personification** (n.)	擬人法
24	**onomatopoeia** (n.)	擬聲法

20 Classical Art—Greek and Roman Art

1	**Classical Art**	古典藝術
2	**influential** (a.)	有影響的
3	**later eras**	之後的年代
4	**pottery** (n.)	陶器
5	**sculpture** (n.)	雕刻品
6	**focus on**	著重在
7	**simplicity** (n.)	簡單；樸素
8	**proportion** (n.)	均衡；比例
9	**architecture** (n.)	建築物；建築風格
10	**column** (n.)	圓柱
11	**classical order**	古典柱式
12	**Doric order**	多立克柱式
13	**Ionic order**	愛奧尼柱式
14	**Corinthian order**	科林斯柱式
15	**base** (n.)	柱礎
16	**shaft** (n.)	柱身
17	**capital** (n.)	柱頭
18	**decorate with**	以……裝飾
19	**spiral** (a.)	螺旋形的
20	**scroll** (n.)	渦卷形裝飾
21	**elaborate** (a.)	精巧的；複雜的
22	**admirer** (n.)	崇拜者
23	**element** (n.)	元素
24	**Coliseum** (n.)	羅馬競技場
25	**symmetrical** (a.)	對稱的
26	**fine** (a.)	優秀的；好的
27	**emphasis** (n.)	強調
28	**well-proportioned** (a.)	勻稱的

21 Classical Music—The Western Musical Tradition

1	**Baroque Period**	巴洛克時期
2	**Classical Period**	古典時期
3	**Romantic Period**	浪漫時期
4	**oratorio** (n.)	神劇
5	**passion** (n.)	熱情；激情
6	**be well known for**	以……著名
7	**religious theme**	宗教主題
8	**complicated** (a.)	複雜的
9	**liveliness** (n.)	活潑；輕快
10	**representative** (a.)	代表性的
11	**be born in**	誕生於
12	**focal point**	焦點
13	**mood** (n.)	曲調
14	**Ninth Symphony**	第九號交響曲
15	**The Marriage of Figaro**	費加洛婚禮
16	**Surprise Symphony**	驚愕交響曲
17	**emotion** (n.)	情感
18	**passionate** (a.)	熱情的；激昂的
19	**fantasy** (n.)	幻想
20	**key aspect**	主要層面

Answers and Translations

01 The Regions of the United States
美國各地區

美國可分為五個地理區域，每個區域都有屬於自己的地形、氣候等自然環境，這些特徵使每個地區互有差別，各異其趣。

美國東北部包括 11 個州和首都華盛頓特區（哥倫比亞特區），主要地形是大西洋沿岸平原和山脈。東北部地區通常又分為新英格蘭、中大西洋地區兩個子區域。

美國歷史上，許多來自歐洲的首批移民定居在東北部，新英格蘭即以逃離英國國教的清教徒，和其他清教徒的早期殖民地而聞名。美國幾個人口密度最高的區域和最大的都會區，也都集中在中大西洋地區，如紐約市、華盛頓特區和費城。

美國東南部包括 12 個州，密西西比河流經此區西部。東南部氣候溫暖、生長季長，適合農民種植許多不同種類的經濟作物。早期殖民耕地擁有者最早生產的經濟作物是菸草和棉花；對現今東南部農民而言，喬治亞州的桃子、陽光普照的佛羅里達州所盛產的柳橙，為其兩大重要經濟作物。

美國中西部多平原和草原。在北美大平原和中央平原上，眼底所見的盡是綿延不絕的肥沃玉米、大豆和麥田，這個地區以此景遠近馳名。密西西比河的源頭與五大湖區的四座大湖均位於中西部，平坦的土地和肥沃的農田使這個地區成為美國的農業中心，人們常稱中西部為「美國的糧倉」。

美國西南部包括亞利桑那州、新墨西哥州、德克薩斯州和奧克拉荷馬州。西南部有許多乾燥地帶及山區，因此形成了數個沙漠。這裡也有許多高原、大峽谷、臺地和孤峰，位於西南部的大峽谷，即為美國最著名的地形之一。

最後，美國西部包含加利福尼亞州、內華達州、奧勒岡州、華盛頓州和山州。阿拉斯加州和夏威夷州雖然屬於西部地區，卻不位於美國本土。西部地區是個擁有眾多不同自然環境的多元化區域，西北部以太平洋沿岸的長海岸線著稱；西南部非常乾燥且有許多沙漠；而山州則大部分由落磯山脈盤據。

- **Vocabulary Preview**

1 **cash crop** 經濟作物　　2 **dominate** 高聳於；俯視

3 **fertile** 肥沃的；富饒的　　4 **arid** 乾燥的

5 **diverse** 多樣的；多元的

- **Quick Check**

1 **(T)**　　2 **(F)**　　3 **(F)**

- **Main Idea and Details**

1 **(c)**　　2 **(c)**　　3 **(a)**　　4 **(b)**

5 a. **urban**　　b. **Midwest**　　c. **Hawaii**

6 a. **Northeast**　　b. **Southwest**　　c. **Mountain States**
　　d. **populated**　　e. **range**

- **Vocabulary Review**

1 **physical environment**　　2 **landforms**　　3 **Arid**

4 **dominated**　　5 **stretches**

02 A Nation of Diversity
美國：民族的大熔爐

美國有時被稱為移民國家，許多來自不同國家和種族的人民定居在此。美國花費了數個世紀才成為一個多元文化社會。美國人民並非同時從世界各地湧來，事實上，美國的移民潮發生在數個不同階段。

克里斯多夫·哥倫布於西元 1492 年發現美洲大陸之後，許多歐洲人開始動身前往美洲。最早抵達美洲大陸的歐洲人有英國人、德國人、愛爾蘭人、荷蘭人和法國人。許多非洲人接踵而至，但他們卻是以奴隸的身分被迫來到美洲大陸。

接下來在西元 1880 到 1924 年間，第二波移民潮湧入美國。這些新移民有許多來自南歐和東歐國家，包括義大利、波蘭和俄羅斯。自 1800 年代晚期，從中國、日本、韓國和其他國家來的亞洲移民，陸續移入美國西部。

第一批移民通常分散在鄉村地區；晚期移民則集中在城市區域。舉例來說，第二波移民潮中，人數最龐大的義大利和猶太族群多集中在紐約和波士頓，芝加哥則匯聚了各種種族和國籍的移民。

如今，美國公民幾乎涵蓋了各國人種，但並非所有民族都能融洽相處，這些移民有時面臨種族歧視。早期的移民，如英國殖民者、愛爾蘭人和德國人，擁有許多共同的英國文化；然而，晚期移民則有許多相異之處，他們說不同的語言，有不同的宗教信仰和習俗。一些已在當地安定下來的人，並不歡迎更多的貧窮新移民到來，也因此形成了對黑人、猶太人、亞洲人和其他種族的社會歧視，直至 1900 年代仍未消滅。

然而，美國政府在 1960 年代通過了廢除種族歧視的法案，如今所有人民不分種族都能享有公平待遇，因此多數美國人已能和諧共處。

- **Vocabulary Preview**

1 **ethnic group** 族群　　2 **concentrate** 集中；聚集

3 **immigrant** 移民　　4 **discrimination** 歧視

5 **stream** 流動

- **Quick Check**

1 **(T)**　　2 **(T)**　　3 **(F)**

- **Main Idea and Details**

1 **(b)**　　2 **(c)**　　3 **(a)**　　4 **(c)**　　5 **(b)**

6 a. **Europe**　　b. **African**　　c. **Eastern**　　d. **religions**
　　e. **Asians**

- **Vocabulary Review**

1 **As a result**　　2 **fairly**　　3 **in harmony**

4 **streamed into**　　5 **concentrated in**

03 From Farming to Technology
美國經濟：從農作到科技業

所謂經濟，是指商品和服務的生產及分銷方式。國家經濟包含了一國境內所有生產者與消費者的活動，一個強盛的經濟可產出無數商品和服務。

美國是現今全球國內生產總值最高的國家。國內生產總值，是指一個國家在一年內所有商品與服務的總產量，擁有全世界最高的國內生產總值代表美國是全球第一大經濟體。

美國早期的經濟發展根基於農業，在西元 1600 到 1700 年代間，絕大多數由歐洲前來美洲的殖民者都是農人。製造業和服務業是後來主要的經濟結構。如今，金融業、科技業是經濟上成長最為快速的產業。

在美國，人民和公司都是自由市場經濟的一部分。在自由市場機制下，人們可自由選擇要生產、購買什麼。農夫可選擇種植何種農作物；工廠經營者可決定生產何種商品；商店老闆可決定銷售何種商品；而當消費者決定購買商品和服務時，他們會考慮機會成本，政府不會干預人民賺錢和花錢的方式。美國經濟也以自由企業制度為基礎，這代表著人人都可擁有、經營自己的企業，這些開創並經營自己事業的人被稱為「企業家」。

大多數情況下，販售商品或服務的商人會根據供需法則來決定價格，如果供給大於需求，價格通常會下降；如果供給小於需求，價格通常會飆漲。

- **Vocabulary Preview**

1 **free market** 自由市場　　2 **opportunity cost** 機會成本
3 **entrepreneur** 創業者；企業家
4 **distribute** 分發；分銷　　5 **interference** 干涉；干預

- **Quick Check**

1 **(F)**　　2 **(T)**　　3 **(F)**

- **Main Idea and Details**

1 **(c)**　　2 **(a)**　　3 **(b)**　　4 **(a)**
5 a. **It stands for gross domestic product.**
　 b. **They are the finance and technology industries.**
　 c. **It is a system in which people own and run their own businesses.**
6 a. **farming**　　b. **Finance**　　c. **GDP**　　d. **business**
　 e. **Demand**

- **Vocabulary Review**

1 **distribute**　　2 **interference**　　3 **scarce**　　4 **based on**
5 **free-enterprise**

04　The Native People of North America　北美洲原住民

約莫一萬五千年以前，最早一批原住民抵達美洲大陸，許多考古學家認為他們是從亞洲跨越陸橋而來。

在冰河時期，亞洲和北美洲有一條狹長的陸地相連，大量的獸群會從亞洲橫越這塊陸橋前來覓食，最早的原住民就是跟著這些供應他們食物的動物來到美洲。在狩獵期間，他們也會採集野生莓果、核果、果實作為食物，這就是為什麼我們會稱這群原住民為「採獵者」。

經年累月下來，越來越多人橫越陸橋到達美洲，廣泛分布於美洲各地，這些人即為美國原住民的祖先。隨著時間過去，早期美洲原住民開始種植食物和建造房屋。他們四處定居，建立起屬於自己的文明。

許多美洲原住民部落開始適應當地環境，部落的文化根據周遭的氣候和自然資源來發展，也正因如此，每個部落的生活型態迥然不同。

北美大平原區聚集了蘇族和拉科塔族等部落，他們以獵捕水牛為食，在土地上到處流浪。他們居住在一種叫做梯皮的圓錐形帳棚，方便他們四處遷徙。

普韋布洛族和納瓦霍族生活在美洲西南部，適應了沙漠裡嚴峻乾燥的環境。普韋布洛族使用一種名叫旱耕法的方式在沙漠裡耕作，並用泥磚建造一種稱為「普韋布洛」的房屋，泥磚可以使房屋免受於炎熱和嚴寒的氣候侵襲。

在西部地區，阿拉斯加的因紐特人捕鯨為食，並以鯨魚皮製衣。特林吉特人是高超的手工藝家，他們利用木頭製作圖騰柱、獨木舟和工藝品。

東部的易洛魁族使用森林裡的素材建造長屋，一些部落甚至結盟組成「易洛魁聯盟」，這些部族是最早與初來美洲的歐洲殖民者有貿易往來的美洲原住民。

- **Vocabulary Preview**

1 **archaeologist** 考古學家　　2 **hunter-gatherer** 採獵者
3 **wander** 漫遊；遊蕩　　4 **alliance** 結盟；同盟
5 **herd** 畜群；牧群

- **Quick Check**

1 **(F)**　　2 **(T)**　　3 **(T)**

- **Main Idea and Details**

1 **(c)**　　2 **(c)**　　3 **(a)**　　4 **(c)**
5 a. **animals**　　b. **adobe**　　c. **Iroquois**
6 a. **land bridge**　　b. **hunter-gatherers**　　c. **buffaloes**
　 d. **Tlingit**　　e. **Confederacy**

- **Vocabulary Review**

1 **herds**　　2 **civilizations**　　3 **ancestors**　　4 **wandered**
5 **settled in**

05　The Age of Exploration　大航海時代

西元十五世紀，許多歐洲國家，如葡萄牙、西班牙、法國、英格蘭，皆與亞洲有商品貿易往來。印度和中國的金礦、絲綢與香料在歐洲需求甚鉅，歐洲人也樂意以高價換取亞洲的商品。不過，商人從陸路到達亞洲的路程十分遙遠，歐洲人於是開始尋找前往亞洲的新路線。

歐洲人競相探訪前往亞洲的海路，由葡萄牙打前鋒，他們發展出一種叫做「卡拉維爾帆船」的新式船艦，相較於其他船隻能駛得更遠更快。西元 1418 年，葡萄牙航海家亨利王子開始派遣探險隊到非洲西岸。葡萄牙人緩慢而平穩地越駛越南，最後，在西元 1487 年，葡萄牙船長巴爾托洛梅烏·狄亞士，成為首位航行至非洲大陸最南端好望角的歐洲人，但他並沒有進入印度洋。約莫十年之後，瓦斯科·達伽馬一路從歐洲航海到印度，歐洲人因而發現了通往亞洲的水路。

葡萄牙人靠著繞行非洲航行到亞洲，但是義大利人克里斯多夫·哥倫布卻認為，可以靠著向西航行，橫跨大西洋到達亞洲。哥倫布說服西班牙國王費迪南和皇后伊莎貝拉，資助他三艘船來完成這項任務，並在西元 1492 年率領這三艘名為平塔號（Pinta）、尼尼亞號（Niña）和聖瑪莉亞號（Santa María）的船啟航。數星期後，他的船員看見陸地，但那卻不是印度大陸，而是「新大陸」，哥倫布因此發現了南北美洲。

西元 1519 年，一支由費迪南·麥哲倫所率領的船隊自西班牙出發，麥哲倫在菲律賓遇害，但他的船員在 1522 年完成了首次環繞地球的航行。隨後，法國、荷蘭和英國相繼參與這場全球大探險的競賽。

十五、十六世紀期間，歐洲對亞洲的航海探險就此改變了全世界，我們稱這個時期為「大航海時代」或「地理大發現」。

- **Vocabulary Preview**

1 **sponsor** 資助；贊助　2 **caravel** 卡拉維爾帆船

3 **expedition** 探險；遠征　4 **circumnavigation** 環球航行

5 **mission** 任務

- **Quick Check**

1 **(F)**　2 **(F)**　3 **(T)**

- **Main Idea and Details**

1 **(c)**　2 **(a)**　3 **(b)**　4 **(c)**　5 **(b)**

6 a. **demand**　b. **land**　c. **Caravels**　d. **Good Hope**

　e. **India**

- **Vocabulary Review**

1 **steadily**　2 **sponsor**　3 **set sail**　4 **willing to**

5 **round**

06 The Spanish Conquerors in the Americas 西班牙人征服美洲

　哥倫布發現美洲大陸之後，越來越多西班牙人前往新大陸，多數是為了尋找當地的金銀財寶，好讓西班牙成為歐洲最富裕的國家。雖然美洲原本就有原住民，但西班牙人卻罔顧當地人的權益。

　西元十六世紀，中、南美洲有兩個主要的帝國，一個是阿茲提克帝國，位於現今的墨西哥；另一個是印加帝國，位於現今南美洲的祕魯。阿茲提克和印加國都有豐沛的金礦和財寶，為西班牙人所覬覦。

　為了在南美洲建立殖民地，西班牙必須先征服阿茲提克。西元 1519 年，埃爾南多·科爾特斯率領了約 550 名征服者乘船前往墨西哥。僅過數年，西班牙人就在 1521 年攻陷阿茲提克的首都特諾奇提特蘭，終結了阿茲提克帝國。十年後，西元 1532 年，另一位西班牙征服者法蘭西斯克·皮薩羅率領一支僅有 185 名士兵和 37 匹馬的探險隊，征服了印加帝國。

　阿茲提克人驍勇善戰，印加人也擁有強壯的體魄，究竟是何原因，能讓士兵數量極少的西班牙在這場戰爭中獲得勝利呢？西班牙人除了擁有火力較強的武器，如槍支、火砲跟盔甲，他們也騎馬作戰，這是美洲原住民前所未見的。西班牙人還有一項更致命的武器──疾病，他們帶著像天花這類可怕的疾病來到新大陸，美洲原住民對天花沒有免疫力，成千上萬的人染病死亡。結果，西班牙人輕易地擊敗大部分的美洲原住民部落，而後奴役這些原住民並奪取他們的財寶。西班牙也在南北美洲佔領許多領土，並且設立殖民地。

- **Vocabulary Preview**

1 **claim**（根據權利）要求；索取　2 **smallpox** 天花

3 **conquistador**【西】征服者　4 **immunity** 免疫力

5 **colony** 殖民地

- **Quick Check**

1 **(T)**　2 **(F)**　3 **(F)**

- **Main Idea and Details**

1 **(c)**　2 **(c)**　3 **(a)**　4 **(c)**

5 a. **They were in search of gold, silver, and other treasures.**

　b. **The two major Native American empires were the Aztec Empire and the Inca Empire.**

　c. **He had 185 men.**

6 a. **capital**　b. **horses**　c. **weapons**　d. **horses**

　e. **Smallpox**

- **Vocabulary Review**

1 **deadly**　2 **Smallpox**　3 **set up**　4 **proceeded to**

5 **claimed**

07 The First French and English Colonies 法國和英國在美洲的首批殖民

　當西班牙人將主要的海外遠征目標集中於中南美洲時，其他歐洲人則探索了北美洲，並在此殖民。在北美洲東岸，兩個最重要的殖民國家分別是法國和英格蘭。

　法國主要的探勘區域在今日的加拿大。西元 1534 年，雅克·卡蒂埃沿著聖勞倫斯河航行；其他的法國探險家，如拉薩爾，則探索了北美內陸。拉薩爾發現了密西西比河，並聲稱其為法國的領土；西元 1608 年，山穆·德·尚普蘭在現今的魁北克建立了一個永久的法國居留區。

　英國勢力主要在大西洋沿岸的大陸東部紮根，西元 1607 年，第一個永久英國居留區設立在維吉尼亞州的詹姆士鎮。這些殖民者為了追求財富而來，渴望致富。然而那裡並沒有黃金，許多移民死於飢荒和疫病。幸虧有殖民地領袖如約翰·史密斯等人的幫助，史密斯曾獲得當地印地安酋長的女兒寶嘉康蒂挺身相救，詹姆士鎮在其協助下逐漸壯大繁榮。

　西元 1620 年，另一個重要的英國殖民地於現今的麻薩諸塞州建立，由一批欲脫離英國國教迫害的英國清教徒所開拓。他們搭乘五月花號（Mayflower）於麻薩諸塞州的普利茅斯上岸，為了宗教信仰而離開英國。

　其他一些英國殖民地居民，也跟隨著這些移居到北美的英國清教徒的信仰，這群人就是後來的清教徒（Puritan）。這些清教徒跟搭乘五月花號前來的英國清教徒一樣，都是極為虔誠的基督徒，而這些清教徒後來在今日麻薩諸塞州的波士頓定居。

　在接下來的一個世紀間，越來越多人由歐洲前往美洲，大部分來自英格蘭，但也有從法國、荷蘭和其他國家來的人。這些移民最後在大西洋東岸建立了十三個獨立殖民地。而後，這些殖民地成為美國初創時期的十三州。

- **Vocabulary Preview**

1 **Puritans** 清教徒　2 **permanent** 永久的

3 **settlement** 殖民地

4 **colonize** 移居於殖民地；開拓殖民地

5 **prosper** 繁榮；昌盛

- **Quick Check**

1 **(F)**　2 **(T)**　3 **(F)**

- **Main Idea and Details**

1 **(c)**　2 **(a)**　3 **(b)**　4 **(a)**

5 a. **Jacques Cartier**　b. *Mayflower*　c. **Boston**

6 a. **St. Lawrence**　b. **Quebec**　c. **Jamestown**

　d. **Massachusetts**　e. **religious**

- **Vocabulary Review**

1 **founded**　2 **settlers**　3 **colonized**

4 **prosper**　5 **eventually**

08 The American Revolution
美國獨立戰爭

西元 1760 年代，美洲有十三個英國殖民地。所謂「殖民地」，就是由外國政府所管轄的區域。美洲的十三個殖民地由英國國王所統治。

同時在西元 1756 到 1763 年其間，英國和法國爆發了七年戰爭，這場戰爭的勝利為英國贏得了密西西比河以東的土地。然而戰事卻使英國付出昂貴代價，英王喬治三世希望北美十三州人民分攤政府的債務，因此制定了稅法開始對商品課稅，讓殖民地居民大為反彈。

西元 1764 年，英國國會通過《糖稅法》；1765 年通過《印花稅法》，意味著殖民地居民不論買糖、郵票或紙，都必須額外賦稅。這些稅法引發居民的抗議，稱新措施為「不可容忍法案」，並開始抵制英國商品，主張「無代表，不納稅」。北美十三州人民希望能在英國國會佔有席次，但遭到英王拒絕，衝突很快就在英國與殖民地居民間展開。

許多北美居民冀望能脫離英國獨立，居民和英國士兵間的緊張態勢導致西元 1770 年發生了波士頓大屠殺。美國民兵開始接受「命令一下立即應召」的訓練。在西元 1775 年 4 月 19 號，被稱為紅衫軍的英國士兵和美國民兵在麻薩諸塞州的萊辛頓和康科特對戰，這兩次戰役是獨立戰爭的前哨戰。一年後，西元 1776 年 7 月 4 日，大陸會議簽署《獨立宣言》，宣告美國是一個獨立的國家。

喬治・華盛頓被指派為大陸軍隊的指揮官，戰爭初期相當艱困，在西元 1777 年贏得薩拉托加戰役之後，北美人民說服法國和其他歐洲國家對他們伸出援手。戰爭延續多年，美洲人輸贏參半。之後在西元 1781 年，美國陸軍和法國海軍迫使英國陸軍將領康華利斯，於維吉尼亞州的約克鎮投降，戰爭就此結束。兩年後，英國承認美洲殖民地的獨立。

- Vocabulary Preview
1 taxation 課稅；徵稅　2 boycott 杯葛；聯合抵制
3 minuteman （美國獨立戰爭期間）命令一下立即應召的民兵
4 surrender 投降　5 Parliament 英國國會

- Quick Check
1 (T)　2 (F)　3 (T)

- Main Idea and Details
1 (c)　2 (a)　3 (b)　4 (b)　5 (c)
6 a. debt　b. representation　c. Declaration
　d. Yorktown　e. independent

- Vocabulary Review
1 boycotted　2 representatives　3 pay off
4 convince　5 Intolerable Acts

Wrap-Up Test 1

A

1 physical environment	2 densely
3 dominated	4 fairly
5 streamed into	6 interference
7 scarce	8 based on
9 civilizations	10 wandered

B

1 competed	2 willing to
3 deadly	4 claimed
5 founded	6 permanent
7 prosper	8 colonists
9 representatives	10 Intolerable Acts

C

1 族群 f	2 移民 i
3 歧視 j	4 企業家 b
5 考古學家 c	6 採獵者 g
7 探險隊 h	8 環繞（地球的）航行 d
9 西班牙征服者 a	10 殖民地 e

D

1 自然環境	2 乾燥的
3 經濟作物	4 草原
5 肥沃的	6 農田
7 多樣的	8 多元文化的
9 地形	10 工藝品
11 結盟；同盟	12 機會成本
13 供給	14 需求
15 部落	16 香料
17 卡拉維爾帆船；輕快帆船	18 探索
19 西班牙人	20 佔領；奪得
21 永久的	22 殖民地
23 要求；索取	24 清教徒
25 免疫力	26 課稅
27（美國）獨立戰爭	28 獨立
29（英國、加拿大等的）國會	30 聯合抵制

09 The Five Kingdoms of Organisms
生物五界說

生物依其共同特徵來分類，古代科學家將所有生物二分為「植物」和「動物」。然而在顯微鏡發明之後，科學家發現了許多需要分類的新生物。今日，科學家將生物以「界」區分為五大類，分別是「原核生物界」、「原生生物界」、「真菌界」、「植物界」和「動物界」。

原核生物界由構造很簡單的單細胞生物組成，只能使用顯微鏡才可看見。單細胞生物又稱為原核生物，這意味著其細胞內缺乏細胞核。細菌和某些海藻屬於原核生物界，這些生物透過細胞壁吸收養分。

原生生物界（或稱單細胞生物）的生物，也只能透過顯微鏡觀察。它們有些擁有動物特徵；有的則具備植物特徵；有些同時擁有動植物的特徵。多數原生生物是單細胞，但有些則是多細胞，包括似動物的阿米巴和似植物的海藻類。海藻細胞內有葉綠體，可行光合作用自行製造食物。

真菌界的生物是多細胞生物，包括黴菌、酵母菌和傘菌。真菌與植物相似，但是前者不行光合作用獲得養分，而是仰賴其他生物的腐生組織為食。

植物界的成員是無法移動的多細胞生物，包括蕨類植物、苔蘚類植物、開花植物、非開花植物。植物細胞含有的葉綠素使植物呈現綠色，也能讓植物行光合作用製造食物。

動物界的成員是可移動的多細胞生物，包括昆蟲、寄生蟲、魚類、爬蟲類、兩棲類和哺乳類。動物無法自行製造食物，而是食用其他生物如植物和動物，以獲取養分。

- Vocabulary Preview

1 **Plantae Kingdom** 植物界

2 **Protista Kingdom** 原生生物界

3 **microscopic** 微小的；只能用顯微鏡看到的

4 **feed on** 以……為食　5 **multicellular** 多細胞的

- Quick Check

1 **(F)**　2 **(F)**　3 **(T)**

- Main Idea and Details

1 **(b)**　2 **(a)**　3 **(a)**　4 **(b)**

5 a. **absorb**　b. **algae**　c. **food**

6 a. **microscope**　b. **bacteria**　c. **amoebas**
   d. **mushrooms**　e. **Multicellular**

- Vocabulary Review

1 **photosynthesis**　2 **feed on**　3 **classified by**

4 **lack**　5 **classification**

10 The Seven Levels of Classification
七級別生物分類法

我們可能對地球上數百萬計的生物一無所知，如果你發現了一種新生物，你會如何命名呢？又會如何分類呢？許久以前，世界各地的科學家難以溝通研究中的生物，因為他們的語言不同，對同一種生物的稱呼也各異。而瑞典科學家卡爾·林奈解決了這個問題，他將所有生物分為七個級別，以拉丁文命名，好讓所有科學家都瞭解生物的名稱。至今我們仍然沿用林奈系統，做為生物分類的依據。

現今科學家將所有生物分為七個級別，分別為「界」、「門」、「綱」、「目」、「科」、「屬」、「種」，每個級別裡的生物都有特定的共同特徵。

「界」是最高的分類階元，每個「界」細分為數個「門」，每個「門」再細分為數個「綱」等等，越往下的級別，分類越具體明確。

所有的生物體都隸屬於五界之一，這五界包括「原核生物界」、「原生生物界」、「真菌界」、「植物界」、「動物界」。其次的分類是「門」，隸屬於同一門的生物，有著相同的體型呈現，譬如，動物界有 33 個「門」，其一是「脊索動物門」，脊索動物指的是有脊骨的動物。

「綱」、「目」、「科」則進一步將生物分類。脊索動物門下分為數個「綱」，包括「哺乳綱」、「爬行綱」、「鳥綱」、「兩棲綱」和「魚綱」。在「哺乳綱」裡，動物依所吃的食物分屬於各「目」，例如「食肉目」、「食草目」和其他類目的動物。「食肉目」裡又將動物分為許多「科」，包括「犬科」、「貓科」和「熊科」。

最後兩個分類是「屬」和「種」，「屬」是一群緊密相關的生物體；「種」是最精確的分類，裡頭的生物都至少包含一個其他生物所沒有的特徵。

生物的歸類決定了它的學名，一般來說，當科學家欲具體說明一種生物時，他們會使用「屬名」加「種名」。學名的前半部說明此生物是哪個「屬」，後半部解釋是哪個「種」，例

如人類的學名是 *Homo sapiens*（智人），*Homo*（人）是「屬名」，*sapiens*（有智慧的）是「種名」。

總的來說，生物分類法提供許多生物資訊，使人們能夠留意到各種生物間的異同。

- Vocabulary Preview

1 **specify** 具體說明　2 **phylum**【生】門

3 **related** 有關的；有親緣關係的　4 **genus**【生】屬

5 **precise** 準確的；確切的

- Quick Check

1 **(T)**　2 **(T)**　3 **(F)**

- Main Idea and Details

1 **(b)**　2 **(b)**　3 **(a)**　4 **(c)**　5 **(b)**

6 a. **classification**　b. **Order**　c. **Family**　d. **related**
   e. **characteristics**

- Vocabulary Review

1 **determine**　2 **depends on**　3 **specify**

4 **take care of**　5 **basis**

11 Plant Structures and Functions
植物構造和功能

植物皆有基本需求，它們需要陽光、水、空氣和養分來生存成長。為了達到這些需求，所有植物都具有一些相同功能的構造。

植物的根部能把植物支撐在地面上，使植物固定在土裡，避免移動。根部也負責從土壤中吸收水分和礦物元素。根的構造使植物吸取水分、礦物，並運送到植物的其他部位。

大部分的植物有細小的根毛，能從土壤中吸收水分和礦物。水分和礦物通過根的皮層進入木質部，再由木質部往上通到植物的莖，進而運送到植物的各部位。

植物的莖支撐葉片和花朵，有些植物的莖巨大堅硬，例如樹幹；有些植物的莖較小且柔軟，例如花卉的莖。然而，不論何種類型的莖，都具有可支援植物運輸系統的基本構造。莖內的木質部可將水分和礦物從根部往上運送；韌皮部則將養分從植物的葉片運送到植物各部位。

有些植物的莖不僅僅只有運送功能，像馬鈴薯的莖就能儲存養分，以供植物往後使用。事實上，我們吃的馬鈴薯就是它的地下莖。除此之外，仙人掌的莖則能在長期缺水的沙漠環境中貯藏水分。

葉子是植物的綠色部分，葉片之所以呈綠色，是因為含有葉綠素，葉綠素存在於葉綠體，能讓植物進行光合作用。光合作用是植物合成食物的過程，植物需要水、二氧化碳和陽光來進行光合作用。水和二氧化碳在葉綠體內結合後，產生糖分和氧氣，植物再利用這些糖分來生長發育。在光合作用期間，植物會釋放氧氣到空氣中，供其他生物吸收；當動植物呼吸的時候，則會放出水和二氧化碳到空氣中。

- Vocabulary Preview

1 **xylem** 木質部　2 **chloroplast** 葉綠體

3 **anchor** 使固定；繫住　4 **photosynthesis** 光合作用

5 **respiration** 呼吸

- Quick Check

1 **(T)**　2 **(F)**　3 **(T)**

1 (a) 2 (b) 3 (a) 4 (b)

5 a. **The phloem moves food from the plant's leaves to the rest of it.**
   b. **They store food for the plants to use later.**
   c. **It is the food-making process of plants.**

6 a. **ground** b. **the soil** c. **roots** d. **green**
   e. **photosynthesis**

• Vocabulary Review

1 **anchor** 2 **Chloroplasts** 3 **responsible for**
4 **functions** 5 **prevent**

12 Flowers and Seeds 花與種子

多數植物透過花，即植物的生殖器官製造種子，並發育成新植物。

花有雄性和雌性部位，雄性部位產生花粉，雌性部位製造會發育成種子的卵細胞。

雄蕊是花的雄性構造，包括花藥、花絲兩構造。花藥產生花粉粒；花絲是連結花藥和植物的柱形結構。雌蕊是花的雌性構造，有三個結構，頂端是柱頭，可以抓住落在上頭的花粉粒，中段似莖的是花柱，子房是花的基座，內含卵細胞，卵細胞受精後會發育成為種子。

植物產生種子前，必須先被授予花粉。當花粉粒自花藥傳遞到柱頭，授粉作用就產生了，授粉作用可以藉由自花授粉或異花授粉達成。如果花粉被傳遞至同一朵花，就稱為「自花授粉」；如果花粉從一朵花的花藥落到另一朵花的柱頭，就叫做「異花授粉」。這也是花瓣的作用，花瓣是環繞在花朵外面顏色鮮豔的覆蓋物，可以吸引蜜蜂、蝴蝶、蜂鳥或其他動物。當牠們在花叢間移動，花粉就會沾黏在牠們身上，並藉此傳送到其他花朵，這就是許多花朵如何被授粉的過程。

花一旦被授粉，花粉即開始萌發成花粉管，一路往下伸到子房，直達卵細胞，發生受精作用，接著形成種子。種子內包含新植物的胚胎，首先會發育成擁有一個或多個種子的果實，這些種子有許多之後會落到地面，落至地面後，種子可能會發芽長成新植物。

• Vocabulary Preview

1 **pollen** 花粉 2 **germinate** 發芽；生長
3 **reproductive** 生殖的 4 **pollination** 授粉
5 **fertilization** 受精

• Quick Check

1 (F) 2 (T) 3 (T)

• Main Idea and Details

1 (b) 2 (c) 3 (b) 4 (a)

5 a. **reproductive** b. **self-pollination** c. **embryo**
6 a. **Stamen** b. **Pistil** c. **Ovary** d. **stigma**
   e. **cross-pollination** f. **pollen tube**

• Vocabulary Review

1 **pollinating** 2 **germinates** 3 **reproductive**
4 **transfer** 5 **fertilized**

13 Plants With Seeds 種子植物

大多數的植物會產生種子，種子植物主要有兩大類：被子植物和裸子植物。

地球上大部分植物是被子植物，花朵、青草、農作物和多數的樹木皆是。被子植物又稱為開花植物，它們會開花，也會結果實。被子植物的種子外有果實保護。所有被子植物的果實都是由花所發育形成，花是植物的生殖器官。

科學家根據植物種子所具有的子葉數目，將被子植物分為兩大類：「單子葉植物」有一片子葉；「雙子葉植物」有兩片子葉。

被子植物生長於各種氣候環境，遍布世界各地，它們是植物界裡最大的分支。

裸子植物會產生種子，卻沒有花朵和果實，不會包在果實裡，它們的種子長在毬果上。大部分的裸子植物是常綠植物，有狹窄的針狀葉片，其中一類是松柏科植物，包括松樹、西洋杉和柏樹。蘇鐵和銀杏是另外兩種裸子植物。

裸子植物沒有花朵和果實，而是以其他方式繁殖。像松樹等針葉樹，通常樹上有雄性和雌性的毬果。雄性毬果釋放含有精核的花粉粒；雌性毬果製造卵細胞。當花粉隨風傳送，正好落在雌性毬果上時，花粉中的精細胞就會和卵細胞相結合，受精的卵子最後發展成為種子。當種子成熟，雌毬果由樹上掉落，散布在地面上。風或水通常會將種子攜離樹木，待時機成熟，種子就發芽並長成新松樹。

裸子植物是最古老的種子植物，數百萬年前，它們曾是地球上主要的植物種類，如今，裸子植物僅剩約 700 種。

• Vocabulary Preview

1 **monocot** 單子葉植物 2 **angiosperm** 被子植物
3 **seed leaf** 子葉 4 **gymnosperm** 裸子植物
5 **reproduce** 繁殖；生殖

• Quick Check

1 (T) 2 (F) 3 (T)

• Main Idea and Details

1 (c) 2 (b) 3 (a) 4 (c) 5 (c)

6 a. **flowers** b. **fruits** c. **dicots** d. **cones**
   e. **conifers**

• Vocabulary Review

1 **reproduce** 2 **Monocots** 3 **Sperm cells**
4 **dominant** 5 **egg cell**

14 Seedless Vascular Plants and Nonvascular Plants 無種子維管束植物和非維管束植物

大部分的植物利用種子繁殖，但並非所有植物皆如此。有些植物不用種子繁殖，我們可將這些無種子植物分為「無種子維管束植物」和「無種子非維管束植物」兩大類。

維管束植物含有由管狀細胞構成的維管束組織，這些組織使水分和養分能運送至根莖。所有被子植物和裸子植物都是維管束植物，而非維管束植物則缺乏這些組織。

苔蘚植物是最常見的無種子非維管束植物，這些植物利用光合作用自行提供養分。然而，它們缺乏維管束植物所含有的葉脈，因為沒有葉脈，非維管束植物無法長得很高大，只能緊靠地面生長。

蕨類植物是最普遍的無種子維管束植物，它們是非常古老的植物，在數百萬年前一度生長繁盛。蕨類植物的葉子稱為蕨葉，它們從蔓延在地底下的地下莖開始發展。由於含有維管束組織，因此可以長得高大粗壯。

苔蘚植物和蕨類植物不靠種子繁殖，而是利用孢子產生新植物，因此它們的生命週期非常類似，苔蘚植物和蕨類植物的生命週期皆有兩個獨立階段。

讓我們來瞧瞧苔蘚植物的生命週期吧！在第一個階段，苔蘚透過無性生殖製造孢子，孢子囊打開後會釋放孢子，降落在潮濕土地上的孢子生長成新植物，這個階段稱為「無性生殖」。苔蘚植物發育後出現雄性和雌性枝條，雄性枝條製造精子，雌性枝條產出卵子。當水分足夠時，精細胞會游至卵子使之受精。每個受精卵會產生一個長柄，並發展出一個裝滿孢子的莢膜，稱為「孢子囊」。此第二個階段稱為「有性生殖」。蕨類植物的生命週期與苔蘚植物非常相似。

- **Vocabulary Preview**

1 **vascular plant** 維管束植物　2 **seedless** 無種子的
3 **lack** 缺少；沒有　4 **spore** 孢子
5 **asexual reproduction** 無性生殖

- **Quick Check**

1 (F)　2 (T)　3 (T)

- **Main Idea and Details**

1 (a)　2 (c)　3 (b)　4 (a)
5 a. **All angiosperms and gymnosperms are vascular plants.**
　b. **Ferns can grow to be tall because they have vascular tissues.**
　c. **Mosses use spores to reproduce.**
6 a. **tissues**　b. **gymnosperms**　c. **spores**　d. **sexual**
　e. **life cycles**

- **Vocabulary Review**

1 **lack**　2 **Sexual reproduction**　3 **common**
4 **Seedless**　5 **asexually**

15 How Do Plants Respond to Their Environments?
植物如何對環境變化做出反應？

生物皆有適應環境的能力以利其生存，植物也會為了存活，對環境做出反應，但植物的反應通常比動物緩慢。向性和其他對環境刺激的反應，能幫助植物滿足其需求。

植物對外界刺激的反應稱為「向性」。向性有數種，一種是「向光性」。向光性使植物向有光的地方生長或彎曲，以獲取最多的光源進行光合作用。另一種是「向地性」，也就是植物對地心引力所做出的生長反應。植物的根會對地心引力的刺激做出反應，因此它們會往下深入土壤生長，而莖和葉則是往空中生長。「向水性」是植物對水的反應，植物（尤其是根部）會向有水的方向生長。

向性是植物的非自主反應，可以是正向或負向。舉例來說，植物的根會朝地心引力方向往下生長，這就是一種正向地性；莖會遠離地心引力的拉力生長，這就是負向地性。

植物也會使用許多方式以適應環境。譬如，沙漠環境相當乾燥少水，仙人掌和其他沙漠植物因此適應了這種天氣，它們可

以忍受長期缺水，並且把握降雨時將大量水分儲藏在身上。同樣地，有些植物因缺乏陽光，會變成肉食性來適應環境。捕蠅草靠著捕食小昆蟲維生，如此一來，它們就可以獲取足夠養分生存。

- **Vocabulary Preview**

1 **tropism** 向性　2 **stimulus** 刺激
3 **phototropism** 向光性　4 **carnivorous** 食肉的；食蟲的
5 **involuntary** 非自主的

- **Quick Check**

1 (T)　2 (F)　3 (F)

- **Main Idea and Details**

1 (c)　2 (b)　3 (a)　4 (a)
5 a. **slowly**　b. **Tropisms**　c. **carnivorous**
6 a. **responses**　b. **sunlight**　c. **Hydrotropism**
　d. **water**　e. **flytrap**

- **Vocabulary Review**

1 **tend to**　2 **carnivorous**　3 **involuntary**
4 **sustain**　5 **cactus**

Wrap-Up Test 2

A
1 classified by　2 Monera
3 Fungi　4 basis
5 related　6 specify
7 prevent　8 responsible for
9 chloroplasts　10 respiration

B
1 pollinating　2 transfer
3 egg cell　4 dominant
5 lack　6 Sexual reproduction
7 asexually　8 reproductive
9 Monocots　10 sustain

C
1 原生生物界 i　2 只能從顯微鏡裡看到的 j
3 門 e　4 屬 b
5 種 d　6 被子植物 a
7 木質部 g　8 裸子植物 f
9 維管束植物 h　10 向光性 c

D
1 原核生物界　2 真菌界
3 多細胞的　4 分類法
5 非自主的　6 依靠
7 詳細說明　8 處理
9 使固定　10 主要的
11 葉綠體　12 光合作用
13 功能　14 運輸系統
15 韌皮部　16 呼吸（作用）
17 花粉　18 雄蕊
19 雌蕊　20 授粉（作用）
21 受精（作用）　22 種子植物
23 子葉　24 子葉

25 松柏科植物；針葉樹　26 非維管束植物

27 孢子　28 無性生殖

29 向性　30 刺激

16 Understanding Numbers 數字概念

　　我們今日所用的數字稱為「阿拉伯數字」，總共有十個數字 0、1、2、3、4、5、6、7、8、9，阿拉伯數字以十進位系統為基礎。有時我們會看到「羅馬數字」，羅馬數字是羅馬人使用的，並非實際的數字，而是用來表示數字的字母或符號，每個字母代表不同的數值，這些字母及其所代表的數字如下：

| I = 1 | V = 5 | X = 10 | L = 50 |
| C = 100 | D = 500 | M = 1,000 | |

　　如果要用羅馬數字表示更大的數字，有兩個規則：如果一個字母後面接一個等值的或較小的字母，就將它們的數值相加。一個字母不能重複三次以上，故，II 是 1+1，或是 2；III 是 1+1+1，或是 3；VI 是 5+1，或是 6。如果較小字母記在較大字母的前面，就要用較大的字母減去較小的字母，故，IV 就是 5–1，或 4；IX 就是 10–1，或 9；XL 就是 50–10，或 40。這個規則非常複雜，也讓數學運算變得異常地困難，你可以自行想像一下，試著將 CCXII 與 XXXVI 相乘看看。

　　幸好我們目前使用的是阿拉伯數字，用阿拉伯數字解數學題比用羅馬數字簡單得多了。

　　接下來，讓我們再多學一點數字觀念吧！數字可以是正的，也可以是負的，我們可以用數線來表示。在 0 右邊的數字是正的，左邊是負的，0 這個數字既非正也非負。

　　這些數字我們稱之為「整數」。有小數的數字，如 0.2、3.14、10.5，並非整數；$\frac{1}{2}$、$4\frac{3}{4}$ 這種分數和帶分數也不是整數。

　　數線越右邊的數字越大（+5>+3）；數線越左邊的數字越小（-1>-100）。正整數永遠大於負整數（1>-100）。

　　另一個分類數字的方式，是將它們分為偶數和奇數，偶數是以 0、2、4、6、8 結尾的數字，14 是偶數，36 和 42 也是偶數；奇數是以 1、3、5、7、9 結尾的數字，11、53、117 都是奇數。

• Vocabulary Preview

1 **Arabic numeral** 阿拉伯數字

2 **Roman numeral** 羅馬數字

3 **whole number** 整數

4 **odd number** 奇數

5 **positive integer** 正整數

• Quick Check

1 **(T)**　2 **(T)**　3 **(F)**

• Main Idea and Details

1 **(b)**　2 **(c)**　3 **(b)**　4 **(c)**　5 **(c)**

6 a. **decimal**　b. **Romans**　c. **fractions**　d. **Even**
　e. **end in**

• Vocabulary Review

1 **repeat**　2 **categorized**　3 **represents**

4 **decimal system**　5 **odd numbers**

17 Geometric Figures 幾何圖形

　　幾何學是一門研究點、線、角的學問，它也探討能以點、線、角所畫出的形狀與圖形。

　　多邊形是由三條以上線段所組成的封閉平面圖形，依其擁有的邊、角和頂點數量來命名。

　　有三個邊的多邊形叫做三角形，我們依照三角形的邊長和內角為其分類。

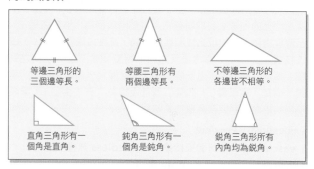

等邊三角形的三個邊等長。　等腰三角形有兩個邊等長。　不等邊三角形的各邊皆不相等。

直角三角形有一個角是直角。　鈍角三角形有一個角是鈍角。　銳角三角形所有內角均為銳角。

　　大小和形狀完全相同的圖形是「全等的」；相同形狀但大小不同的圖形是「相似的」；相似圖形的對應邊長度為「成比例的」。

　　有四個邊的多邊形叫做「四邊形」，四邊形有五個特別的種類：「平行四邊形」、「矩形」、「正方形」、「菱形」和「梯形」。

　　平行四邊形有兩對平行邊，對邊和對角都是相等的。

　　矩形是所有內角皆為直角、對邊等長的平行四邊形；正方形有四個相等的邊和四個直角。

　　菱形是四個邊都等長的平行四邊形，其兩條對稱軸正好在對角線上。

　　梯形也有四個邊，但只有一對平行邊。

　　五個邊的多邊形叫做「五邊形」；六個邊的叫做六邊形。七邊形有七個邊；八邊形有八個邊；九邊形有九個邊；十邊形有十個邊。理論上，多邊形可以有無數個邊，但所有的邊都必須相接，構成一個封閉的圖形。

• Vocabulary Preview

1 **proportional** 成比例的　2 **polygon** 多邊形

3 **congruent** 全等的　4 **parallel** 平行的

5 **line segment** 線段

• Quick Check

1 **(F)**　2 **(T)**　3 **(F)**

• Main Idea and Details

1 **(c)**　2 **(a)**　3 **(c)**　4 **(b)**

5 a. **It is a triangle with three equal sides.**
　b. **It is a parallelogram with all four sides congruent.**
　c. **A hexagon has six sides.**

6 a. **Isosceles**　b. **Scalene triangle**　c. **Obtuse triangle**
　d. **Parallelogram**　e. **Trapezoid**

• Vocabulary Review

1 **axes of symmetry**　2 **line segments**

3 **parallel sides**　4 **proportional**　5 **constructed**

18 The *Iliad* and the *Odyssey*
《伊里亞德》和《奧德賽》

約莫三千年前，古希臘有一位最偉大的敘事家，是個名為「荷馬」的男子。傳說荷馬是位盲眼詩人，他講述了兩個史上最偉大的故事：《伊里亞德》和《奧德賽》。《伊里亞德》和《奧德賽》屬於長篇史詩，內容描述古希臘偉大的英雄、男神和女神。由於荷馬是口傳詩人，因此他的詩到後來才被人們記載下來。

《伊里亞德》敘述特洛伊戰爭的故事，也就是特洛伊與希臘人民之間的長期抗戰。特洛伊王子帕里斯，綁架了希臘人墨涅拉俄斯的妻子海倫——世界上最美麗的女人。所有希臘領袖聯合起來攻打特洛伊，參戰者中有許多傑出的英雄，像阿傑克斯、奧德修斯和阿卡曼農，但最偉大的希臘戰士是阿基里斯，他在戰爭中令人生畏而且所向披靡，腳踝是他全身唯一的弱點。而此時抵禦特洛伊最偉大的英雄則是赫克特。

特洛伊戰爭持續十年，特洛伊城最後被希臘人奧德修斯策畫妙技攻陷。希臘人打造了一隻巨大的木馬，將它放在特洛伊的城牆外，然後假裝離開。特洛伊人將木馬拖進城內，認為是獻給眾神的禮物，殊不知特洛伊木馬內藏希臘伏兵。當晚，希臘士兵溜出木馬，打開城門，最後攻佔特洛伊城。

《奧德賽》述說奧德修斯的歸鄉旅程的故事。特洛伊戰爭結束後，奧德修斯花了十年才回到家鄉伊薩卡，途中遭遇許多艱難險阻，差點被獨眼巨人波呂斐摩斯所殺，還險些被女巫賽絲施法變成豬，他也去過冥界，他的船員全軍覆沒。然而，多虧眾神的幫忙，特別是雅典娜，奧德修斯才得以返家，並受到他忠實妻子潘妮洛普的迎接。

- **Vocabulary Preview**

1 **sorceress** 女巫　　2 **oral** 口述的　　3 **kidnap** 誘拐；綁架
4 **creep** 躡手躡足走；緩慢地行進　　5 **epic poem** 史詩

- **Quick Check**

1 (F)　　2 (F)　　3 (T)

- **Main Idea and Details**

1 (b)　　2 (a)　　3 (c)　　4 (b)
5 a. **Menelaus**　　b. **wood**　　c. **underworld**
6 a. **Trojan War**　　b. **Trojan Horse**　　c. **Odysseus**
　　d. **cyclops**

- **Vocabulary Review**

1 **kidnapped**　　2 **pretended to**　　3 **greeted by**
4 **crept out of**　　5 **devised by**

19 Figures of Speech　修辭

當作家創作文學時，他們會運用「字面性語言」和「比喻性語言」。字義性語言直接傳達字面的意思，許多寫作都會使用字義性語言。然而，很多作家也會使用比喻性語言來寫作，運用比喻性語言能使文章更具創意、增添更多想像空間。作家使用比喻性語言的方式有非常多種。

其中一種方式就是運用「修辭」，修辭是不能直接以字面意義來理解的表現手法。修辭通常讓讀者心中產生意象。「明喻」和「隱喻」是兩種最常見的修辭手法，兩者都屬於「比喻」，但明喻是「直接比喻」，隱喻是「間接比喻」。

此外，明喻通常使用「如同」跟「像」來比較兩種事物。舉例來說，「愛像一朵玫瑰」是明喻；還有許多明喻是用動物形象表達，例如「他像獅子般大吼」和「她如綿羊般溫順」，就是兩個明喻的例子。隱喻的比喻關係不如明喻明顯，它是把兩個看似沒有共同點的事物拿來比喻，也不會使用「像」、「如同」這類字眼。隱喻的例子有「她是我眼裡的蘋果」、「他是一隻驢」、「有一片沙海」。

另一種常見的修辭手法是「擬人法」，擬人法是將人的特質加諸在動物、植物、事物或想法上頭，像「月亮在沉睡」、「隔牆有耳」和「時間不等人」都是擬人法的例子。

有些作家喜歡在作品中使用擬人法，也就是狀聲字的運用，譬如，蛇會「嘶嘶」叫、蜜蜂會「嗡嗡」叫、鐘會「叮咚」響。

- **Vocabulary Preview**

1 **onomatopoeia** 擬聲法　　2 **simile** 明喻
3 **personification** 擬人法　　4 **metaphor** 隱喻
5 **literally** 照字面地

- **Quick Check**

1 (F)　　2 (T)　　3 (F)

- **Main Idea and Details**

1 (a)　　2 (a)　　3 (c)　　4 (c)　　5 (b)
6 a. **animals**　　b. **Metaphor**　　c. **unlike**　　d. **human**
　　e. **Onomatopoeia**

- **Vocabulary Review**

1 **onomatopoeia**　　2 **as obvious as**　　3 **literal language**
4 **employ**　　5 **literally**

20 Greek and Roman Art　希臘羅馬藝術

藝術史上，古典藝術時期是一段對後世極具影響力的年代。古典藝術指的是古希臘羅馬的藝術，古希臘羅馬人創造了許多傑出的藝術作品，包括陶器、雕像和建築。

古典藝術著重「簡單」和「均衡」，古希臘人率先創造了這種風格，他們認為和諧與均衡是藝術最重要的特質。要了解古典藝術最簡單的方法，就是觀察此時期的建築風格。

古希臘人興建建築物，會使用柱子來做支撐，他們會從三種古典柱式中選擇一種來使用，分別為「多立克柱式」、「愛奧尼柱式」和「科林斯柱式」。大多數圓柱底部有柱礎，中間是柱身，頂端有柱頭。多立克柱式是最古老的柱式，造型也最簡單，通常沒有柱礎；愛奧尼柱式的柱頭有渦卷形裝飾；科林斯柱式的柱頭最華麗也最精緻。

羅馬人是希臘藝術的崇拜者，他們複製了許多希臘作品，其中也融入了埃及文化的新元素。

希臘的阿波羅神殿、希拉女神廟和帕德嫩神廟都是古典建築，羅馬則有羅馬競技場跟萬神殿。這些建築都有對稱結構，是古典強調和諧、均衡的佳例。

古希臘羅馬人也創造了許多美麗的雕像，他們偏重自然美與人體的和諧，將人體描繪成勻稱、和諧的體態。像希臘雕刻家米隆所創作的《擲鐵餅者》及《美景宮的阿波羅》，都是展現人體之美和勻稱體態的佳例。

- **Vocabulary Preview**

1 **Ionic order** 愛奧尼柱式　　2 **Doric order** 多立克柱式
3 **symmetrical** 對稱的　　4 **depict** 描寫；描繪
5 **proportion** 比例；均衡

• Main Idea and Details

1 (b)   2 (c)   3 (b)   4 (a)

5 a. It focused on simplicity and proportion.

　b. They were the Doric, Ionic, and Corinthian orders.

　c. They depicted it as a well-proportioned and harmonious form.

6 a. Greece   b. simplicity   c. columns

　d. spiral scrolls   e. capitals

• Vocabulary Review

1 focused on   2 columns   3 depicted

4 influential   5 symmetrical

21 The Western Musical Tradition
西方音樂傳統

歷史上有許多音樂時期，其中最著名的是「巴洛克時期」、「古典時期」和「浪漫時期」，這些時期的作曲家創作出古典音樂史上的偉大樂章。

巴洛克時期大致在西元 1600 年至 1750 年之間。約翰·塞巴斯提安·巴哈和喬治·弗里德里克·韓德爾名列巴洛克時期最偉大的作曲家。這個時代產生許多新的音樂類型，如歌劇、神劇和受難曲。此時期常偏重宗教音樂，巴哈和韓德爾即是以創作宗教題材的音樂而廣為人知。巴哈譜寫的《馬太受難曲》，韓德爾創作內含《哈利路亞大合唱》的《彌賽亞》，都屬於宗教作品。巴洛克音樂通常十分複雜、難演奏，並以節奏活潑著稱，韓德爾的《水上音樂》和《皇家煙火》即為本時期代表作品。

下一個偉大時期稱為古典時期，時間約從西元 1750 年到 1825 年。這時期享譽最盛的三位作曲家分別為沃夫岡·阿瑪迪斯·莫札特、約瑟夫·海頓和路德維希·凡·貝多芬，他們都出生於奧地利維也納，也因此讓維也納成為此時期的焦點。古典音樂比起巴洛克音樂要來得柔和簡單許多。不同於巴洛克音樂，古典音樂的曲調常於一首樂曲內多作變化，曲子也較短。奏鳴曲和交響樂在古典時期十分普遍，貝多芬的《第九號交響曲》、莫札特的《費加洛婚禮》和海頓的《驚愕交響曲》都是當時受歡迎的作品。

浪漫時期從西元 1815 年到 1910 年，這時期的作品通常傳達強烈情感，聽起來顯得澎湃激昂，奇幻和想像是此時作曲家寫曲的主要層面。比起古典音樂時期，這個時期有更多樂器加入管弦樂隊一同演奏。許多浪漫時期的樂曲都相當長，例如理察·華格納的作品。浪漫時期著名的作曲家有法蘭茲·舒伯特、羅伯特·舒曼和弗雷德里克·蕭邦。

• Vocabulary Preview

1 piece 曲；篇   2 Baroque Period 巴洛克時期

3 passionate 熱情的；激昂的   4 compose 作曲

5 Classical Period 古典時期

• Quick Check

1 (F)   2 (T)   3 (T)

• Main Idea and Details

1 (c)   2 (b)   3 (a)   4 (a)

5 a. Bach   b. symphonies   c. instruments

6 a. Bach   b. religious   c. Beethoven   d. symphonies
　e. Chopin

• Vocabulary Review

1 compose   2 focal point   3 opera

4 representative   5 passionate

Wrap-Up Test 3

A

1 Arabic numerals   2 represent

3 categorized   4 decimal system

5 odd numbers   6 axes of symmetry

7 proportional   8 pretended to

9 crept out of   10 almost

B

1 Literal language   2 literally

3 comparisons   4 Personification

5 influential   6 focused on

7 Ionic   8 Corinthian

9 admirers   10 focal point

C

1 整數 h   2 複雜的 c

3 幾何學 d   4 全等的 f

5 四邊形 b   6 比喻性語言 g

7 隱喻 j   8 女巫 e

9 口述的 a   10 史詩 i

D

1 十進制   2 被……迎接

3 從……爬出   4 由……所設計

5 正整數   6 多邊形

7 無限的   8 傳說

8 令人生畏的   10 擬聲法

11 像……一樣明顯   12 使用

13 照字面地   14 圓柱

15 有影響的   16 對稱的

17 代表性的   18 熱情的；激昂的

19 明喻   20 擬人法

21 修辭手法   22 愛奧尼柱式

23 多立克柱式   24 科林斯柱式

25 崇拜者   26 均衡；比例

27 巴洛克時期   28 浪漫時期

29 古典時期   30 焦點

FÜN學 美國英語閱讀課本 7
各學科實用課文

Authors

Michael A. Putlack
Michael A. Putlack graduated from Tufts University in Medford, Massachusetts, USA, where he got his B.A. in History and English and his M.A. in History. He has written a number of books for children, teenagers, and adults.

e-Creative Contents
A creative group that develops English contents and products for ESL and EFL students.

作者	Michael A. Putlack & e-Creative Contents
翻譯	丁宥暄
編輯	丁宥榆／丁宥暄
校對	陳慧莉／申文怡
製程管理	洪巧玲
發行人	周均亮
出版者	寂天文化事業股份有限公司
電話	+886-(0)2-2365-9739
傳真	+886-(0)2-2365-9835
網址	www.icosmos.com.tw
讀者服務	onlineservice@icosmos.com.tw
出版日期	2020 年 9 月 二版再刷 (080202)

國家圖書館出版品預行編目 (CIP) 資料

FUN 學美國英語閱讀課本：各學科實用課文 / Michael A. Putlack, e-Creative Contents 著；丁宥暄, 鄭玉瑋譯. -- 二版 . -- [臺北市]：寂天文化，2017.02- 冊；公分

ISBN 978-986-318-552-9 (第 1 冊：平裝附光碟片)
ISBN 978-986-318-554-3 (第 2 冊：平裝附光碟片)
ISBN 978-986-318-559-8 (第 3 冊：平裝附光碟片)
ISBN 978-986-318-566-6 (第 4 冊：平裝附光碟片)
ISBN 978-986-318-567-3 (第 5 冊：平裝附光碟片)
ISBN 978-986-318-578-9 (第 6 冊：平裝附光碟片)
ISBN 978-986-318-581-9 (第 7 冊：平裝附光碟片)

1. 英語 2. 讀本

805.18   106001668